"W... I kissed you right now?"

"What?"

"I want to kiss you," Matthew said.

Chanté renewed her efforts to escape his embrace, but her wild bucking and squirming only succeeded in increasing the rising tension between them.

When his lips landed on hers with surprising gentleness, Chanté's mutinous body melted. Their tongues danced, caressed and sent small shock waves of pleasure clear down to her toes. She wanted him and could tell he wanted her, too.

She could give in just this once. What would be the harm? After all, they were still married. And Like it or not, she still loved him and probably always would.

"Tell me you want me," he commanded softly.

I want you, Chanté thought. She met her husband's fevered gaze while a war raged inside her. She could bend and be flexible. But she knew that giving in to him tonight wouldn't magically erase their problems....

Books by Adrianne Byrd

Kimani Romance

She's My Baby
When Valentines Collide

Kimani Press Arabesque

Defenseless
Measure of a Man
Deadly Double
The Beautiful Ones
When You Were Mine

ADRIANNE BYRD

has always preferred to live within the realm of her imagination, where all the men are gorgeous and the women are worth whatever trouble they manage to get into.

ADRIANNE *BYRD*

When *Valentines Collide*

KIMANI
ROMANCE

This book is dedicated to the new angel on my shoulder—
Alice Coleman Finnley. I can still hear your laughter.

 KIMANI PRESS™

ISBN-13: 978-0-373-86005-0
ISBN-10: 0-373-86005-6

WHEN VALENTINES COLLIDE

Copyright © 2007 by Adrianne Byrd

www.kimanipress.com

Printed in U.S.A.

Dear Reader,

I hope you enjoy *When Valentines Collide*. This was rather an interesting subject matter for me to explore. Over the years, I've watched my share of talk shows and listened to psychiatrists, legit and self-described alike. I don't really trust people who claim to know all the answers. And I've learned from the queen of talk shows—Oprah Winfrey—that people who seem to have perfect lives usually have more problems than the people trotting across the stage for Jerry Springer and Maury Povich. This got me thinking: what if Oprah and Dr. Phil were married? And better yet, what if in private they couldn't stand each other? These were the original questions that filtered across my mind before I asked myself how I could also work in great sex for this angry couple. Then it hit me: *sex therapy.*

Now, I'm not a doctor, but I can write about them in romance novels. And sex therapy sounds like it will fix just about any problem to me. At the very least, it should be fun!

Chapter 1

"He's an egotistical, self-righteous son of a bitch," Chanté Valentine spat, storming through her best friend and publishing editor, Edie Hathaway's front door. "The man thinks he's God's gift to psychology."

"Please, come in," Edie mumbled in the wake of her trail, sighed, and then closed the door. Shaking her head and tightening her belt around her curvy, plus-size figure, she followed her friend back into the dining room.

"I can't do this any longer," Chanté announced as she marched straight toward the bar.

"It's eight in the morning."

"What can I say? I like vodka with my eggs."

Edie patiently watched her bestselling author splash out a glass of her expensive liquor. "You could add a dash of orange juice so I'd feel better about you getting something nutritional out of that drink."

Chanté smirked, but complied. "I want a divorce."

"Absolutely not." Edie crossed her arms. "It would ruin both of your careers."

Chanté downed a deep gulp and then came up for air. "I don't care."

"Sure you do." Edie shuffled over to the table where her breakfast grew cold. "Besides, you still love him…or you would've left him a long time ago."

"Ha! I've been trying to leave Matthew for the last two years, but it's always 'wait until after contract negotiations, wait until after you write your book, wait until after the book is published.'

Now the blasted thing has been number one on the *New York Times* bestseller list for ten weeks running and you're still telling me to wait."

"You *should* wait." Edie shook her head as she slathered butter onto a biscuit. "How would it look if America's two top relationship gurus divorced each other? Don't you think we would have a credibility issue here?"

"Oh, give me a break." Chanté downed a second gulp. "If I didn't know any better, I'd think you, Seth and Matthew have all teamed up to drive me nuts."

"All right." Edie lowered her biscuit without taking a bite. "I know I'm going to regret asking, but what did Matthew do this time?"

One of Chanté's brows rose quizzically. "I take it you didn't watch Letterman last night?"

"Tivo. I'd planned to watch it this morning," Edie said, sounding concerned. "Why? What happened?"

Chanté's eyes narrowed as she simmered. "Letterman snidely pointed out the differences in our approaches in relationship counseling and then asked how people should choose whose advice to follow."

Edie leaned back in her chair and brushed back her thick straw curls from her face. "And...what did he say?"

"That people should follow the advice from the one who graduated from a *real* school."

Edie's mouth rounded silently.

"You should have seen him sitting there as proud as a peacock, cramming his overpriced education down everyone's throat." Chanté sloshed her drink down onto the breakfast bar and flailed her hands in the air. "Oh, look at me. I'm a Princeton graduate while my wife—"

"Graduated from Kissessme College in Karankawa, Texas," Edie finished.

"Which is a damn good school," Chanté snapped. "I busted my butt with two waitressing jobs to get my degree. I didn't have a rich daddy to write me a blank check."

Edie frowned. "I know you two are going through a rough patch—"

"This is more than a rough patch."

"But sometimes I wonder how the hell you two got together in the first place."

"Oh, that's easy." Chanté strode to the table and pulled out a chair. "Ten years ago, Matthew Valentine was handsome—"

"He still is."

"Charming—"

"Check."

"Successful."

"Double-check."

Chanté's lips curled wickedly. "And *great* in bed."

Edie's eyebrows rose with surprise and interest. "Oh?"

"Now he seems to think all he has to do is get his groove on and wait for a baby. A baby. That's all he ever talks about. After nine miscarriages you'd think he would give it a rest." Chanté drew a deep breath.

"So I take it you haven't told him you're—?"

"How can I?" She sloshed down another gulp, exhaled, and then finally slumped her shoulders in defeat. "Nine miscarriages. Five years. I should have started trying to have a family earlier."

"Come on. You wanted a career first. That's understandable."

"Yeah, but now I'm pushing forty and my body attacks every fertilized egg like I've caught a disease or something." She shook her head. "I can't help but wonder if I'd tried sooner I'd already have our baby as opposed to being on this wild race against my biological clock—a race Matthew is determined to win." Chanté shook her head during another sigh. "I just need a break—physically and emotionally."

"Is that why you kicked him out of your bedroom?"

"How did you—?"

"Seth." Edie filled in the blanks. "He'll never admit it, but those two gossip more than we do. If I remember correctly it's been…what—five months?"

Chanté took another gulp. "Something like that."

Her friend shook her head as she folded her arms and leaned back in her chair. "You know you're playing with fire when you let too much testosterone pile up. Not to mention, you seem a little wound tight yourself."

"If I'm wound too tight it's because I'm frustrated that Matthew and I can fix everyone's marriage problems but our own."

"That's because it always boils down to the battle of the wills with you guys." Edie shrugged and then returned her attention to her breakfast. "Both of you always have to be right."

Chanté grew indignant. "That's not true…entirely."

Edie continued eating.

"The problem is that two perfectionists should never marry each other."

"Or two stubborn people."

"Edie! You're supposed to be on my side."

"I'm on reality's side." Her friend finally cast her a long look. "It's not going to kill you to bend a little."

"If I bend any further you may as well remove my spine," Chanté snipped.

"Better flexibility can only improve one's sex life." Edie winked. "I can testify to that."

"I just bet you can."

* * *

Once a month, Dr. Matthew Valentine and his agent, Seth Hathaway, met at the International House of Pancakes for their favorite selection of Rooty Tuitty Fresh and Fruity pancakes.

"It was a joke," Matthew laughed, and then leaned toward Seth. "It was Letterman, for Pete's sake."

Seth leaned his six-foot-five frame over the table and settled his serene ocean-blue eyes on him. "Let me guess, Chanté didn't think it was funny?"

"Blew a damn gasket is more like it," Matthew rolled his eyes. "For punishment, I endured a four-hour rant about how I was undermining her authority and poking holes in her credibility—*not* the first time I heard that crap by the way." He stabbed his pancakes and twirled it absently in its strawberry syrup. "There's no pleasing her anymore."

Seth kept his face blank as he bridged his hands above his plate. "Far be it for me to give America's top relationship guru advice."

Matthew glanced up wearily. "But something tells me I'm not going to be able to stop you."

"Hey, I don't have a fancy degree, but twenty-five years of marriage—an interracial marriage at that—says I'm qualified."

Matthew flashed his million-dollar smile and forced a casual shrug. "All right. Shoot."

Seth waited until he'd captured Matthew's full attention. "Apologize."

Matthew waited for more, but concluded none was forthcoming when his agent returned his attention to his breakfast.

"That's it?"

"Yep." Seth shoveled food into his mouth.

Matthew rolled his eyes. "Good thing I didn't call you for help during the writing of my last book."

Seth smiled and dabbed the corners of his mouth. "C'mon. It's not rocket science. A man is just fooling himself if he thinks he could ever win an argument with a woman. Everything is always our fault. I don't care what it is. So apologize and move on."

"I didn't do anything wrong."

"You're joking, right?" Seth rocked back in his chair as his laughter rumbled. "Look, I don't mean to offend you or anything. I mean, you're my best client and all, but, when a woman gets mad it's usually for three reasons: something we did, something we didn't do or something we're going to do."

"Sounds scientific."

"Thanks. It is." He took another bite and quickly swallowed. "In *this* case, you went on a nationally televised show and made a lousy sucker punch to her reputation. Every man watching knew you'd get the couch last night."

"You don't understand." Matthew slumped back in his chair and refused to give credence to Seth's advice. "Once upon a time Chanté didn't take everything so seriously. She knew how to laugh at herself. C'mon. She graduated from Kissessme College. That's funny."

"She also has a syndicated talk radio show and is a bestselling author."

"I know about her accomplishments. I'm proud of what she's done—"

"So it's not so hard to understand she just wants to be taken seriously in her profession."

Matthew shook his head. "I'm telling you, I know my wife. She's not mad about something I said on Letterman. There's something else that's bothering her and she just won't spit it out."

"She keeps asking for a divorce," Seth reminded him.

Matthew shook his head again. "She doesn't want a divorce or she would have been gone by now. It's something else—I'm sure of it. She just won't talk to me."

"Two psychologists who can't talk. I think that falls under irony."

"Very funny."

Seth chuckled. "How long now since the Love Doctor has been locked out of his own bedroom?"

Matt grunted and lowered his gaze.

"Five months, right?" the agent continued, during Matt's silence. "Look, you're a big shot in your field—four number one *New York Times* bestsellers and a syndicated television talk show, but maybe it's time you listen to advice other than your own. *Apologize* and move back into your old bedroom. If you don't, things between you and Chanté are only going to get worse."

Chapter 2

Chanté breezed into WLUV's studio with her head held high but with her lips showcasing a nervous smile. The station's small crew greeted her with wide toothy grins, however, no one's eyes managed to meet hers. To top it off, on more than one occasion, she heard snickering whenever she turned her back.

"Oh, don't pay it any mind," Thad Brown, Chanté's extremely young, talented and laid-back producer advised as he settled behind the glass partition separating them and reversed his New York Yankees baseball cap.

"Easy for you to say," Chanté mumbled, and then placed on her headset.

"To be honest, I thought it was pretty funny," Thad said into his microphone. "Of course, I'm a little hurt I didn't know this embarrassing tidbit about you. I thought we were best friends."

"Thad—"

"Yeah, yeah. I forgot. You have a *new* best friend—a hotshot publishing editor."

"Thad," she warned.

"Okay. Okay." He shrugged with a lopsided smile. "But when you start hobnobbing with Oprah…call me."

"First, I'll have to call my mother."

"You're on a hot streak. Hell, I bought your book yesterday and I'm halfway through it. Real good stuff. A lot better than—well, it could have been professional jealousy that sparked Dr. Matt's comment on Letterman the other night. Did you ever think of that?"

The On Air sign lit up.

"A little competition will do Matthew Valentine a world of good. Maybe his loyal readers will actually demand he write new material instead of rehashing the same trivial tripe of his last three books." She laughed and rolled her eyes. "And don't get me started on those Jerry Springer rejects he says he counsels on his show."

Still laughing, Chanté lifted her eyes to Thad and was stunned to see him frantically pointing upward. When her gaze landed on the sign, her voice failed her.

Static filled the airwaves.

Thad cringed and rolled his hands, urging her to speak.

"Good evening…and welcome to *The Open Heart Forum.* I'm thrilled you could join us. I am your host and friend, Dr. Chanté Valentine. If you're trying to salvage a relationship or if you're experiencing trouble moving on, I urge you to pick up the phone and talk to a friend."

Thad slumped back into his chair and sighed in relief.

With her nerves still tied in knots, Chanté settled into a groove.

From the computer screen on her desk, she read Thad's notes regarding her first caller and launched into her introduction. "Hello, Maria. Welcome to *The Open Heart Forum*."

"Hello, Dr. Valentine." A young, giddy voice filtered on to the line. "I can't believe I actually got through. I have to tell you, I read your book, *I Do,* and I'm a big fan."

"Why, thank you." Chanté smiled. "What's on your heart tonight?"

"Uhm…actually, I was wondering if everything was all right with you and *your* husband—The Love Doctor?"

Chanté blinked and glanced up.

Thad grimaced, shrugged, and then mouthed an apology.

Chanté forced a chuckle. "Yes. Yes. Everything is wonderful between Matthew and I."

"Oh. Well, I didn't think much about it when I saw Dr. Matthew on Letterman, but then I heard you a few minutes ago…?"

"No. No. I was just joking with Thad, my producer. Everything is fine," Chanté lied.

"Well, it just sounded like—"

"Maria, I'm reading here you called in about a friend of yours?" She kept her voice sugary sweet.

"Well, yes. You."

Chanté frowned. "I don't understand."

Maria laughed. "Don't you always encourage your listeners to view you as our friend?"

"Yes. Yes. Of course." Chanté covered quickly. "And thank you, Maria, for your concern. But I assure you, Matthew and I are fine. Thank you for your call." She disconnected the line and then returned her attention to the computer screen.

"Okay. Our next caller is Sienna. She's calling in from Decatur, Georgia. Hello, Sienna, what's on your heart tonight?"

"Hello, Dr. Valentine. I'm a first-time caller and longtime fan."

"Welcome to the show."

"Thank you. I just have one question."

Chanté relaxed. "Sure. What can I help you with?"

"I was looking on the Internet and I couldn't find anything about Kissessme College. Is that a real school?"

Chanté glared at her producer and slid her finger across her neck to let him know exactly what she was going to do when she got her hands on him.

"I'm going to kill her!" Matthew swore as he toted his autographed Reggie Jackson baseball bat and paced the spacious foyer of their multi-million-dollar home.

Their *dream* home. Ha! It was more like a palatial prison—one of their making.

"Maybe I imagined it," he reasoned, but then shook his head. His wife had turned on him on national airwaves. He couldn't believe it. "I should just give her that damn divorce."

Anything would be better than a public castration.

"Jerry Springer rejects," he mumbled under his breath. "I ought to—"

The front door rattled. Matthew stopped in

front of the foyer's threshold leading toward the living room and turned to watch the door. As it crept open, he adjusted and readjusted his grip on the bat.

"Matthew?" Chanté's voice floated through the cracked door.

Waves of anger rushed up the column of his neck.

"Matthew?" she tried again, but didn't dare step into the house. "I know you're in the foyer. I can see you through the side paneling."

His shoulders deflated now, the element of surprise had been taken from him.

"What are you going to do with that bat?"

He'd almost asked "what bat?" when he became cognizant of what he must look like. "I think better with it." He placed the bat next to a crystal vase on the foyer table. "As much as I want to kill you, I'm not interested in doing the time."

As soon as he spoke those magic words, Chanté pushed the door open farther and entered the house.

Despite his anger, Matthew's gaze traveled up

his wife's long, toned legs and black, mid-thigh skirt. Boy, she always did know how to wear the hell out of a skirt—or anything else for that matter. Just months away from the big 4-0, Chanté labored to maintain her Tyra Banks-like figure and there wasn't a man who'd crossed her path that didn't take a moment to appreciate all her hard work—including him.

His eyes continued their journey over her every luscious curve until they reached her thin, delicate neck. He sighed as he envisioned wrapping his hands around it.

"You're still up," she stated the obvious as she closed the door.

"Was there any doubt?" He drew another deep breath in hopes to cool his temper. "How was work tonight?"

Chanté set her briefcase down next to his baseball bat. "It was all right." She shrugged as she pulled the pins from her hair.

Matthew's heart squeezed at the sight of her long, thick, currently dyed auburn hair spilling down her back. Sidetracked, he struggled to remember the last time he ran his fingers through the soft strands—or tugged it during the throes of passion.

Five months.

She headed toward him and had almost passed by when Matthew broke through his reverie and jutted his arm across the threshold to block her escape.

"Surely it was more than just 'all right'?"

Chanté swept her dark, angry glare over him.

Heat flared anew within Matthew, but it had nothing to do with anger. Standing this close, staring into her fiery eyes, and smelling the soft fragrance in her hair, he was delirious with lust.

This made no sense. He couldn't stand her.

Five months.

"Move out of my way," she hissed.

"I want to talk more about your evening," he hissed back, and then added a smile. "Isn't that what all *loving* couples do—communicate?"

"We're not a loving couple so let's just skip the bull." She ducked under his arm and stormed to the bar. "And if you want to talk about that little

comment I made about you on the air tonight…"
She stopped and flashed him a smile. "It was a
joke."

His anger returned. "A joke my ass. You did
that to get back at me. Admit it."

Chanté folded her arms across her chest. "And
what if I did? What are you going to do about it—
divorce me?"

"Don't tempt me!"

Frustrated, Chanté stomped her foot and
glanced around the room to throw something—
anything. She grabbed a nearby statue, but was
stunned when the damn thing wouldn't move.

"What the—?"

"Superglue," Matthew replied with a smug
smile. "Your screaming tirades have gotten a little
on the expensive side."

Big, bright patches of red flashed before her
eyes and she reached for something else, only to
discover it, too, had been glued down.

Her husband laughed, plunging deeper under
her skin. In a last desperate act, she pulled off a
shoe and hurled it at him.

Matthew ducked. "Hey!"

She launched the second shoe and it nailed the side of his head.

"Ouch!" He rubbed his bruise and then took off running toward her. "You've lost your mind."

Chanté squealed as she lunged from him. "Get away. Leave me alone." She bounded up on the sofa and rushed across its cushions.

"I'm going to make you pay for that."

"Don't you dare touch me!" She jumped down, slid on her stocking feet, then raced in the opposite direction.

Matthew crashed into a bookcase and yelped in pain when a few hardcovers landed on his head. "Damn it!"

Chanté glanced over her shoulder as she exited the living room. To her surprise, her husband was right on her tail. She'd crossed the foyer and was just inches away from the staircase, when his strong fingers bit into her shoulders.

"Gotcha!"

Chanté swung as she pivoted.

Matthew ducked, lost his balance, and fell

backward—taking her down with him. He landed with a hard thump and had no time to register the pain before his wife knocked what little air he had left out of his lungs.

In no time, her hands and legs flailed out in attack.

"Will you stop it?" He wrestled with her, trying to catch hold of her.

"I hate you. I hate you. I hate you."

He latched on to one arm, but failed to catch the other one before it landed a hard blow against the same spot her flying shoe had hit. "Ouch!"

Matthew captured the other hand. He rolled on top and pinned her beneath him.

Even then Chanté kicked and squirmed.

"Be still," Matthew demanded.

"Go to hell," she spat.

"What? This isn't 666 Hell's Drive?"

"Very funny." She gave a last futile tug, and then went limp beneath him.

"Give up?"

"Never."

Her chest heaved while she dragged in deep

breaths. It, consequently, drew her husband's lustful gaze. It was crazy, but she felt good lying beneath him—her curvy body soft but pulsing with raw energy. He was turned on—and she knew it.

Five months.

"What are you doing?" she asked in alarm.

He leaned down close until their faces were just inches apart. He filled his senses with her floral-scented hair and the faint hint of Chanel No. 5.

"What will you do if I kiss you right now?"

"What?"

"I want to kiss you."

Chanté renewed her escape efforts, but the wild bucking and squirming only succeeded in turning them both on more.

When his lips landed on hers with surprising gentleness, Chanté's mutinous body melted as though cold water had been splashed onto a fire.

Their tongues danced, caressed, and sent small shock waves of pleasure clear down to her toes. She wanted him, and judging by the hard bulge in his pants, he wanted her, too.

She could give in just this once. After all, it had been five long months. What was the harm? God knew she still loved him—probably always will.

"Tell me you want me," he commanded softly. "We don't even have to go upstairs. We can do it right here. Right now, but I want to hear you say it."

I want you. Chanté panted and tried to gain control of herself.

"Tell me."

She met her husband's fevered gaze while the war continued to rage inside of her. Bend—be flexible. But giving in to him wouldn't magically erase their problems.

"Who knows, tonight might be the night…"

A baby. She closed her eyes. *Always a baby.* Forcing ice into her veins, Chanté lifted her chin, and with her next words extinguished the small fire crackling between them. "I want you to get the hell off of me."

Chapter 3

Matthew didn't sleep a wink.

How could he when all he could think about was marching down the hall to the master bedroom—his old bedroom—and demand his wife perform her wifely duties?

Fat chance.

He chuckled under his breath and watched as the sunlight beamed through the thin slits in the venetian blinds. The rays warmed his face but he wondered when it would touch his heart.

This was not supposed to be his life.

He was never the type of man who trembled at the idea of settling down, having the white picket fence or having the customary two point five children...

Children.

Coming from a large family of four brothers, four sisters and a host of cousins, nieces and nephews, Matthew had always assumed that one day he, too, would raise a small army of children. He'd originally delayed those plans to support his wife in her career. But when they actually started planning five years ago, there was a snag. Chanté could get pregnant, but ten weeks into the pregnancies, like clockwork, her body would reject the fetus.

Five years. Nine miscarriages. Nine heartbreaks.

Matthew swung his legs over the side of the bed and sat up. Children were what was missing from their home—from their lives. He knew it, she knew it and all their friends knew it, too.

And yet, it wasn't in the cards for them.

He sighed; mourned for the children he didn't have, and then reached for his copy of Chanté's latest book, *I Do*. "Following an argument, we need time to cool off. When one person hisses a sarcastic comment and the other, hurt and angry, feels justified in topping the insult. The volleys begin. By the time we realize the mistake we're making, it's too late to 'take it back.'"

He slapped the book closed and hung his head in shame. Seth was right. "I should have apologized."

A loud rip caught his attention and he jerked his head toward the door. When he heard it again, he frowned and went to investigate. Upon opening the bedroom door, he couldn't wrap his brain around what he was seeing.

"What in the hell are you doing?"

Dressed in sexy, silk pink boxers and a matching lace chemise, Chanté stood with a large roll of duct tape and a pair of scissors. "What does it look like I'm doing?"

"It *looks* like you've lost your mind." He took another glance at the silver duct tape running down the center of the floor, the wall, and even the ceiling. "Do you know what's going to happen when you peel that off?"

"I'm not going to peel it off." She huffed. "Since a *real* divorce doesn't suit either of our interests—at the moment—it doesn't mean that we can't go ahead and divvy things up."

He heard her and his brain replayed what she'd said, but it still wasn't making a lick of sense.

"Split everything in half," she clarified at his look of confusion. "Fifty-fifty."

Matthew crossed his arms over his bare chest and leaned against his bedroom's doorframe. "You don't think people might notice? I mean, the tape clashes with the furniture."

"Then we won't invite anyone over," she settled, turning on her heels and marching away.

"You're joking, right?" He started after her.

"No."

He reached the top of the staircase just as she bolted from the bottom of it. "Can we please talk about this like two rational adults?" he shouted.

"I'm through with being rational."

"Obviously."

Chanté stopped and glared up at him. "I'm tired of this lie—this life. I'm tired of…"

He sucked in a deep breath as his eyes narrowed on her. "Go ahead. Say it."

Chanté clamped her mouth shut and stormed away.

Matthew descended the stairs two at a time, ignoring the ugly silver tape down the center. "Say it, Chanté."

She ignored him and continued toward the kitchen. It, too, had been duct taped in half. The sight of it ignited his anger.

"You have something to say, Chanté. I want to hear it."

"Since when?" She rounded on him.

He stopped within inches of her. "I'm standing right here."

Their glares fused as they stood in a stalemate.

"What else are you tired of, Chanté?" he asked.

"You." She lifted her chin, now that she'd said the word. "I'm tired of having to deal with you. Satisfied?"

"Quite." Matthew turned and stomped out of the kitchen.

Chanté watched him leave with a wave of regret and relief. She had no explanation as to why she baited him. She also didn't understand why she was so angry all the time. She could psychoanalyze herself. After all, she was a professional; but the truth is: doctors made terrible patients.

Why couldn't she just say what was really on her mind? Because it would destroy him. She shook her head and turned toward the sink and filled a glass with water, where she proceeded to take her morning vitamins and pills.

The phone rang and Chanté snatched the cordless from the kitchen's wall unit. "Hello."

"What on earth did you do?" Edie asked in a high, strained voice. "No, scratch that. I know what you did. I need to know why you did it."

Chanté sighed as she pinched the bridge of her nose. "You're talking about last night's program?"

"Are you kidding?" Edie's voice rose another

octave. "That's all everyone is talking about. My boss has left six messages on my voice mail. She's worried how all this is going to affect your book sales."

"Edie—"

"Not to mention, my assistant has fielded calls from the big three networks. Even *The Enquirer* called and stated they're going to run a story about you two not sleeping in the same bedroom."

"How did they—?"

Something loud roared from outside. Chanté lowered the phone. Was Matt doing something in the yard? She placed the phone back against her ear.

"—we're going to have to do some damage control on this thing."

"Edie, let me call you back."

"No. We need to talk about this now."

Chanté peeked out of the kitchen window and didn't see her husband.

"Seth and I have a few ideas. What do you think about going on *Larry King Live?*"

"What? Are you sure all of this is necessary?" Chanté headed toward the front door.

"Vital. If this doesn't work, we'll have to sell our souls to get you on Oprah."

Chanté opened the door, screamed and dropped the phone. "Stop! Stop!"

Now dressed in protective clothing, Matthew headed toward his wife's brand-new Mercedes with a chainsaw.

"What are you doing?" she yelled.

"Divvying our assets, hon." He smiled as he lowered his goggles and proceeded to cut the car in half.

"Stop, stop!" she screeched, but the loud buzz of the chainsaw drowned her out. Chanté raced toward the car, but jumped back before sparks showered onto her flammable outfit. "You're crazy," she shouted and stomped her fluffy pink house slippers.

Matthew didn't spare a glance in her direction, but he smiled like a kid in a candy shop as the saw cut through the car like warm butter.

Chanté charged toward the garage, looking for something—anything. From the corner of her eye she spotted a pile of steel pipes on Matthew's workbench and quickly grabbed one before returning to the yard.

The chainsaw jammed halfway through the Mercedes' roof and Matthew climbed down, wondering if he had something stronger to finish the job when he saw an angry pink blur rushing toward him and he removed his goggles.

With a firm grip on the steel pipe, Chanté swung at her husband's head like Barry Bonds going for another home run record.

Matthew ducked and felt the air swoosh past his head as he dropped the chainsaw.

The force of the swing twisted Chanté around in a complete circle and before she could adjust, her husband charged and tackled her to the ground.

This time the air was knocked out of Chanté's lungs as the steel pipe bounced out of her hands.

"What the hell were you trying to do—kill me?" Matthew barked.

"Damn right," she growled and tried to twist away and reclaim the pipe.

"Oh, no you don't." Matthew scrambled above

her and pushed the pipe further out of reach. "You're absolutely certifiable. You know that?"

"Me?" she shrieked. "Look what you did to my car!" Chanté squirmed and then started pelting him with her hands—a constant occurrence, especially in the last six months.

While the wrestling match grew fast and furious in the grass, the sprinklers came on and immediately drenched the couple from head to toe.

"My hair," Chanté sputtered. "I just had it done. Let me up!"

Matthew tried, but the grass was slippery now and he had a hard time getting his footing.

"Get up!" she insisted, smacking him again.

After one too many pops against the head, Matthew waved a finger at her. "Has anyone ever told you that it's never okay to hit?"

Her answer was to smack him again.

"Uh, excuse me."

Chanté and Matthew froze, and then slowly turned their heads to see old man Roger, the lawn guy, peering curiously over at them.

"Uh, is everything all right, Mr. and Mrs. Valentine?"

Their smiles were instant and their expressions as innocent as they could manage.

"Everything is f-fine," Matthew said, finally climbing off his wife and pulling her up with him. For a few strained and awkward seconds they stood before the elderly gentleman in the sodden grass while the sprinklers continued to drench and plaster their clothes against their bodies.

"Uh-huh." Roger eyeballed them as if they were Martians.

Chanté snuggled against her husband and slid her arms lovingly around his neck. "We were just trying something new. You know…to keep things…fresh." She planted a kiss on Matthew's cheek. "Isn't that right, hon?"

Matthew's smile tightened. "Right…hon."

Roger's dusty brown face wrinkled as he scratched his short-cropped, cotton-white hair. "Uh-huh."

"Well, hon," Matt said. "I think we better move this lovefest back into the house." Before Chanté had a chance to respond, Matthew swept up his wife, tossed her over his shoulder, and smacked her hard on the butt.

"Matthew!" Her fist pounded his back.

"Patience, baby." Matthew winked at Roger. "She gets a little impatient from time to time."

"Right." Roger nodded as he watched Matthew march toward the house. From behind, Chanté lifted her head and waved.

At last, Roger turned toward the Mercedes. "Hey, what happened to the car?" He glanced back to his employers, but they were already entering the house.

Mrs. Valentine screeched. "Now put me down!"

The door slammed closed, leaving Roger to scratch his head and glance from the car to the front door. "I swear those two are as loony as they come."

Chapter 4

Master interviewer, Larry King, dressed in a starched periwinkle shirt, black suspenders and matching striped tie performed his trademark haunch over the desk and welcomed the audience to the night's show.

"It's always a pleasure to welcome Dr. Matthew and Chanté Valentine to the show. Dr. Matt is the host of the highly-rated TV talk show, *The Love Doctor*. He is the author of four *New York Times* bestsellers…"

Matt smiled and scratched at his collar.

Chanté drew a deep breath and forced steel into her spine while keeping her smile on full wattage. This interview called for her finest performance.

Matt shifted in his chair, scratched his arm and then jerked the arm to scratch at his back.

Mr. King flashed Matt an inquisitive glance but kept on with his spiel.

"And this little lady, Dr. Chanté Valentine, has quite a résumé as well," Mr. King praised. "She is the host of her own syndicated radio talk show *The Open Heart Forum.* Her first book, *I Do*—I have the book right here—has been on the bestseller list for ten weeks running. Welcome to the show."

"Thank you." She smiled and leaned closer toward her husband.

Matt jerked his head back and tried to scratch at his neck, his chest, his back and his crotch.

"Is everything all right, Dr. Valentine?"

"Oh, uh. Yeah, just fine," he panted, jerking this way and that. "I just seem to have a little itch."

Chanté smiled serenely, thinking about the itching powder she'd sprinkled in his clothes. *That'll teach him to destroy my car.*

Off set, Edie and Seth Hathaway took turns experiencing chest pains as they watched the Valentines attempt to charm their host, but watching them was like watching and expecting a train wreck.

"This was a mistake," Edie whispered and glanced nervously around.

"This is damage control. We needed to do something other than let them continue taking public potshots."

"Look at her. She looks like a plastic Stepford wife and he…what the hell is he doing?"

"Calm down." Seth looped an arm around her shoulder. "They're doing fine. Look, Larry is eating it up."

"Larry is the least of our worries. It's the court of public opinion that matters here." She hid her face in the palms of her hands. "Why did she have to call his TV guests Jerry Springer rejects?"

Seth chuckled. "Because some of them are."

"What?"

"You didn't know?" He shook his head. "You're probably the only one who didn't."

"Well, we wouldn't have to do any damage control if your client reined in his jealousy on Letterman."

"C'mon. If you graduated from a place called Kissessme, you should grow a thick skin."

Edie stepped away from her husband. "Are you saying all of this is Chanté's fault?"

Stagehands, cameramen and the director glanced toward them and Edie realized she'd forgotten to use her "inside" voice. "Sorry," she whispered to the set.

On camera, the Valentines smiled lovingly at each other and their host. But then Matt started raking at his skin like a madman again.

"I'm not saying that it's anyone's fault," Seth resumed the conversation. "But I do think we're sitting on top of a time bomb. We may be able to fool the public right now, but how long do you think they'll be able to keep it up?"

Edie thought of Chanté's constant demand for a divorce. "Not much longer."

"Right." Seth's voice lowered. "Which is why I think it's up to us to do something about it."

"Us?" She laughed. "How are we going to help professional psychologists—the top in their field, by the way—mend their own relationship?"

Seth's lips slid into a wide grin. "An intervention."

"An intervention?" Edie repeated and turned her gaze back to Chanté and Matt, just as Matt twisted one too many times and fell out his chair, then proceeded to writhe on the floor. "Forget the intervention, I think we need an exorcist."

"Oh, *hell* no," Chanté snapped at Edie above the den of diners at the prestigious Gramercy Tavern. When all eyes shot to their table, Chanté quickly covered with a bland smile, and then added under her breath, "I'm not going to marriage counseling."

Unfazed by her friend's outburst, Edie calmly peered over the rim of her glasses. "If you look me in the eye and tell me that you honestly want a divorce, I'll back off."

Chanté opened her mouth to make her daily proclamation, but when the words failed her, she closed it and shifted in her chair.

A triumphant smile bloomed across Edie's lips. "I didn't think so."

"Explain to me how it would look for two relationship experts to seek relationship counseling. Wouldn't that also put a dent in our precious credibility?"

"The public will never know," she assured.

"Come on. We live in the information age." Chanté stabbed at her spinach salad. "Secrets always come out—usually on the Internet."

Edie slumped back in her chair, thoughtful. "Then we could release the information ourselves." She bobbed her head, warming to the idea. "Hear me out on this." She sat up again. "You and Matthew promote counseling. What better way to show that all relationships hit rough patches? Right now, you guys appear to have the perfect marriage. There are a good percentage of people who think you guys can never understand their problems because you have it so good. But if they see perfect marriages being not-so-perfect then we can tap into a few more readers."

"What are you talking about? People see those marriages all the time. They're called celebrity marriages.".

"Be serious. No one takes celebrity marriages seriously. We're talking about two famous love doctors, and when you fix their marriage, it will renew hope."

"*If* we can fix our marriage." Chanté bit into her salad and rolled her eyes. "And that's a very big if."

"Okay. We'll keep it out of the papers for now, but if a leak happens we'll be prepared."

Chanté lowered her gaze and stared at her half-eaten salad, remembering the first time she'd laid eyes on Matthew. He'd blown a tire out on the main highway and walked ten miles to Sam's Café on the edge of Karankawa, Texas, where she waitressed. It didn't take a rocket scientist to figure out with his perfect speech, soft manicured hands and expensive shoes that he wasn't from around those parts.

Chanté chuckled aloud from the memory, but

snapped to attention when Edie's sharp gaze zeroed in on her.

The last thing she expected today was to be ambushed with an intervention for her own marriage. However, her own solution to surviving the rest of her life with her self-absorbed, self-righteous and pretentious husband had already cost her a new Mercedes.

However, the question was whether she wanted to fix her marriage. As she struggled for an answer, her vision blurred, but she blinked away the tears and forced down another bite of food.

Edie watched Chanté from over the rim of her glasses for a long time before she prompted, "Well? You have to do something before you kill each other or kill yourselves. You know psychologists have the highest suicide rate."

"Where did you hear that?"

"I read it somewhere."

"Huh. I always thought it was dentists who had the highest rate."

"C'mon. What do you say? Will you go to marriage counseling?"

* * *

Matthew Valentine, handsome in a royal-blue suit, stared over the heads of his studio audience and into the camera. "Today we will be talking about how to take the bitterness out of your marriage." He smiled, but remained serious. "Oftentimes, it's not the big things that break a marriage. It's the small things." His voice quivered and for a brief moment, Matt appeared to have lost his concentration.

Seth shifted his gaze from one of the monitors to glance at his client on the stage.

The ultimate professional, Matthew recovered and continued with his spiel. The irony of today's subject matter didn't escape Seth so he found himself paying close attention to how Matthew interacted with his guests and the advice Matthew gave them.

"Couples tend to argue over something safe or superficial during battle, but they avoid talking about the serious problems."

Seth nodded as he listened. Everything Matthew said was sound advice. Everything made sense to him—so what were the serious problems between Matthew and Chanté? Where had they gone wrong?

While Matthew continued to mingle with his audience and offer handkerchiefs to sobbing guests, Seth thought back to when he first sensed trouble between Matthew and Chanté. Actually, he didn't sense, more like he dodged a glass vase when he'd entered the Valentines' home during a heated argument. Chanté was a small woman but she had one hell of an arm.

Two hours later, with the day's show finally completed taping and the last of the audience filtered out of the studio, Seth made it to Matt's dressing room and lingered just outside the door while a young, petite, yet curvaceous intern fawned over her employer.

"Great show today, Dr. Valentine," she said breathily. "I swear it's like you really know how a woman thinks and feels."

Seth lifted an inquisitive brow.

"Thank you, Cookie." Matt didn't spare the young girl a glance as he stripped the light coat of makeup from his face.

However, Cookie ignored his indifference and stepped forward until her perky bosom brushed against Matt's arm. "I know I've only been here six weeks, but I have to tell you—working with you has been like a dream come true." She reached out a hand and gently stroked the side of his face.

Belatedly, Matt flinched from her touch.

"You're using the cologne I bought you for your birthday."

"Yeah, I decided what the hell. I've been using the same cologne for ten years."

Smiling like a seasoned temptress, she winked. "If there's ever anything you need—I'll be more than happy to help."

Matt finally met her gaze, but didn't respond.

Enough was enough. Seth cleared his throat.

Matt jumped again and then his face flushed a deep burgundy. "Seth," he boomed too loudly. "C'mon in. Cookie, that will be all for today."

The vixen's lips managed to spread wider as she demurely cast her gaze down. "If you say so, Dr. Valentine." She turned and walked saucily toward the door.

"Remember, if you need anything—anything at all—call me." Cookie winked and disappeared from the door.

"Can you spell *trouble?*" Seth asked, blinking from the trance her swaying hips induced.

"Who—Cookie?" Matt asked. "She's harmless."

"So is a starved lion—as long as you're not locked inside its cage." Seth folded his arms and leaned against the doorframe. "Look, Matt. I don't know how to say this other than to just come out and say it."

Matt cast a curious glance at the mirror and met Seth's reflected stare. "All right. Let me have it."

"I think you and Chanté should see a marriage counselor."

A silence roared on the heels of his words and judging by the intense glare from Matthew, he expected the vanity mirror to crack at any second.

"Have you lost your mind?" Matthew asked, standing from his chair and storming toward the door.

Seth managed to jump out of the way before Matt slammed it on his arm.

"Chanté and I are fine. The last thing we need is a marriage counselor," he said and barked a humorless laugh.

Seth glanced around the room and feigned surprise to find there were no other parties surrounding him. "I'm sorry. Are you talking to me—or someone else who hasn't refereed a few screaming matches at your home?"

"All couples have disagreements," Matt answered flatly and then exchanged his starched white shirt for something more appropriate for the tennis court. "Of course, they usually refrain from putting itching powder in each other's clothes."

"Or cutting each other's cars in half."

A wide smile monopolized Matt's face. "That was pretty good." He jutted a finger. "Extreme—but pretty good."

"Come on. What's the big deal?" Seth shrugged. "You encourage and educate people everyday about the importance of counseling. What's the big deal in practicing what you preach?"

Matthew unzipped his pants and jerked them down his legs. "The big deal is there isn't a damn thing that a psychologist can tell us that we don't already know. We're both controlling perfectionists with hot tempers. Theories and overblown rhetoric are not what we need. Especially when you're dealing with someone who is stubborn as an ox."

Seth frowned. "Help me out. Who's the ox in this scenario?"

"Not funny." Matthew tried to pull his left leg out from the bunched pants leg, but instead lost his footing and fell face forward. "Goddamn it."

Seth covered his mouth in time to cork his laughter.

By the time Matthew recovered and climbed back to his feet there was no trace of amusement on Seth's face—despite Matt's sock suspenders and Daffy Duck boxer shorts.

Matthew cleared his throat and then launched into an explanation for the boxers. "Chanté burned just about everything in my underwear drawer after the car incident."

"I think you got off lucky."

At last, Matthew smiled as he reached for his pristine-white tennis shorts. "I do, too."

A knock rapped on the door.

"Come in," Matt shouted.

Cookie peeked inside with a sheepish grin. "Your package arrived, Dr. Valentine."

Matthew's eyes lit up as he clapped his hands together. "Oh. Bring him in."

Seth's brows furrowed in curiosity but the feeling was quickly sated when Cookie entered the dressing room with the most adorable brown-and-white puppy.

"There's my little man," Matt exclaimed, finally stepping free from his trousers to reach for the dog. "Thank you, Cookie."

"My pleasure. Do you know what you're going to name him?"

"I'm not sure yet." Matt scratched behind the puppy's ear. "I have to spend some time with him and get a sense of his personality."

Cookie leaned over and kissed the dog on top of the head. "Well, keep me posted. I love dogs!"

"Will do."

The intern gave either Matt or the dog a wink, Seth couldn't tell which.

"Call if you need anything," she reminded him again and then disappeared with another wink.

"Excuse me, uhm," Seth said once the door closed. "But isn't Chanté allergic to dogs?"

"She's not allergic," Matt said unconcerned. "She just hates them."

"I stand corrected."

Matt sat in his makeup chair and began to coo and imitate baby talk to the bundle of fur.

"What kind of dog is he?"

"Bulldog. Isn't he handsome? Maybe I should name him Buddy? As in *my* Buddy."

"You know your wife is going to hit the roof when she sees him."

"Probably." Matt smiled. "But I'll just keep him on my side of the house. Besides, everyone needs companionship. A fact my wife seems to have forgotten."

Seth stared at his friend. Finally, he decided to stop pussyfooting around. "Let me ask you something. And be honest if you can. If you and Chanté continue on the way you have been, how long do you think it will be before you finally accept Cookie's invitation?"

A flash of anger returned to Matthew's eyes. "You're out of line."

"And you're in denial."

That loud silence returned to the room, but this time it was layered with a tension usually reserved for heavyweight boxers on fight night.

"Look, I'm your friend."

"You're my agent."

Seth thrust up his chin at the verbal blow. "All right. I'm your agent. As your agent I think I should warn you that a marriage counselor is better for your reputation than getting caught with your hands in the *Cookie jar.*"

Matthew's heated black gaze snapped up to Seth as he opened the door.

"Think about it, Matt." His gaze shifted to the puppy. "Good luck, Buddy. Something tells me that you're going to need it."

Chapter 5

"Hello, Shawanda. Welcome to *The Open Heart Forum*."

"Dr. Valentine? Oh, Lawd, girl. I didn't think I would ever get through."

Chanté chuckled as she glanced up at Thad through the glass partition. "Well, I'm glad you did, Shawanda. What's on your heart tonight?"

"Yeah, well, I need to get some advice on what I should do about this (beep!) that's been creeping around with my man."

"Whoa, whoa, Shawanda." Chanté laughed. "I got to tell you this isn't one of those trashy talk shows, so I'm going have to ask you to watch the language. You think that you can do that?"

"Yeah, girl. Just tell me what I should do about this…heifa stalking my man 'cause I'm seriously about to catch a case if she calls my house one more damn time."

"Well," Chanté shook her head and braided her fingers. "Have you confronted your husband about this woman?"

"Oh, we ain't married or nothing. We've just been living together the last fifteen years."

Thad slapped a hand around his mouth while Chanté remained composed.

"I see. Before I address your question, Shawanda—do you mind if I ask you a question?"

"Uh, well, I guess not."

"Why have you wasted fifteen years of your life on a man who clearly doesn't respect you enough to marry you?"

"Hey, that's my baby's daddy. The ring will

come. I mean, you know, he first has to get his wife to sign the divorce papers."

"His wife?"

"Yeah, she's been trippin' ever since he chose me over her trifling behind."

"So let me get this straight—" Chanté straightened in her chair. "You're calling because your man is exhibiting the same behavior you benefited from fifteen years ago when he left his wife for you. Do I understand that right?"

"Look, Rufus left my sister because she didn't know how to treat him right. She never could keep a man, if you know what I mean."

"Unfortunately, I think I do." Chanté sighed. "All right, Shawanda and the rest of you ladies out there who think that hanging on to a man, any man, by any means necessary is the road to eternal bliss. Snap out of it!"

Chanté drew a deep breath and shook her finger at her desk microphone like it was an errant child. "This sort of behavior is unacceptable, despicable and downright counterproductive. It's bad enough that you destroyed one family, but you're calling me to help you stop someone from paying you back for what you put out in the universe. The way I see it, Shawanda, you have two choices, get out or suck it up.

"If you have any sense left you'll do the right thing and crawl to your sister on your hands and knees and beg for forgiveness. Got it?"

A loud click followed by a dial tone filled the airwaves.

"Humph. Another woman who can't take the truth." She shook her head. "Look, ladies. One of the hardest things you'll ever have to learn is to know when to let go. It's not always healthy to only listen to your heart. Your heart can convince you to give up things you have no business giving up. Trust me, I know."

Chanté stayed her tongue, realizing that she'd nearly said too much. To her surprise, Thad had already removed his headphones and was stretched out in his chair, shaking his head.

"We cut to Dr. Laura Schlessinger's repeat show about a minute ago."

"Oh, thank God." Chanté sighed and dropped

her head on her desk. "I was about to experience a serious case of verbal diarrhea."

Thad stood from his chair and strode out of the control room and into the studio booth. "Hey, what do you say we grab some coffee at our favorite diner? We could talk and…talk."

Chanté rolled her head to the side and peeked up at him. "Talk?"

Somehow, she managed to lift her head and smile. "Thanks, Thad…but I think I'm going to have to take a rain check." She removed her headset.

He nodded with obvious disappointment. "All right. But I got to tell you—the rain checks are stacking pretty high. I'm going to start cashing them in soon—real soon."

"Tomorrow?"

"Tomorrow night it is." Thad slid the bill of his Yankees cap to the front and winked. "Get some rest. You look like you need it."

Chanté watched the young producer as he shuffled out of the studio and then felt herself tumble back into a void so complete, she barely had any energy to pack up her belongings. "Sleep," she mumbled under her breath. "What a novel idea."

Like a zombie, she headed out to the employee parking lot. Despite exhaustion, Chanté knew when she climbed into bed, sleep would be rationed out in fitful doses. Such had been the case for the past five months. Ever since she'd kicked Matthew out of their bedroom.

She was angry. He was angry. She threw things. He shouted hurtful things at the top of his lungs. Neither apologized. To do so would mean that one of them was wrong. After eleven years of marriage, Chanté was tired of always being wrong.

Chanté's heels clicked louder against the asphalt, renewed anger brewed in her blood. Over the past five months, she'd lamented over every argument they had ever had and not once had Matthew apologized.

Not once.

As she approached her parking space, the sight of the rented Mercedes only fed her anger.

Matthew deserved more than just some itching powder sprinkled in his clothes—maybe being thrown into a cage with a wild animal would elicit some sense of satisfaction.

"Okay, maybe that's a little too harsh," she admitted, but a smile curved her lips all the same.

As Chanté merged into traffic, she wished that she'd taken Thad up on his offer for coffee and a talk. She wanted to talk to someone, but hated feeling pressured to do so. The irony of that didn't escape her.

She drove for hours, most of the time going back and forth over the same stretch of highway—never really ready to make the right exit for her house. No matter the hour, she knew Matt would be waiting up for her in the living room, although he would never admit it. He'd always claimed to be working whether his laptop was on or not. That still meant something, didn't it? What about the other night when he'd nearly made love to her on the floor of the foyer?

Wasn't that a sign that he still wanted her?

At least her body...or what her body should be capable of giving him.

A child.

The white lines of the road blurred at the sudden sting of tears. Why couldn't Matt just let it go? Not every couple had children. Not everyone was meant to be parents.

But in the last six years her husband had grown obsessed. From endless tests to new and innovative positions, Matthew was determined to have a child. Making love had become sex and sex had become a dull, emotionless act that had left her feeling more empty and dissatisfied than when they started.

Matt never noticed. After all, to a man, an orgasm was an orgasm.

Chanté reached the point that she didn't even bother faking it anymore. And if she wasn't enjoying it, then why do it?

Still, the other night, an old familiar spark had flared between them. Or had she imagined it? She mulled the question over a moment, but in the end was no closer to an answer than she was that night.

But I wanted to make love to him.

That was an inescapable fact.

After a marathon of hot and sweaty sex, Edie and Seth curled into a nice spoon while they waited to catch their next wind.

"God, you're beautiful," Seth panted, peppering his wife's back with butterfly kisses.

"You just make sure you don't forget it," Edie purred and wiggled her rump against his growing erection.

Seth laughed but reached over and snatched a white Kleenex, a surrender flag, from the night-stand and waved it in front of his wife. "I give up. I can't go on without the aid of a medic."

Edie groaned and then inched out of their beloved spoon to roll over and face him. "You know if you keep conking out on me, I just might have to get myself a younger man."

"Then I'll just have to get myself an older woman. Someone who knows how to roll over and go to sleep after four rounds."

"Better not." Edie giggled before she laid

another long, hot kiss on him. When she pulled away, she gazed deep into his eyes. "Promise me that we'll always be like this."

"I promise that we'll always be like this."

"Even when I grow old and my skin gets all wrinkly?"

"Even then."

"Even when my hair turns all gray and I'll have to put my teeth in a glass next to the bed?"

"Ooh, no teeth, huh? That could come in handy."

Edie popped him on the arm. "Promise."

Seth chuckled and drew her soft body close. "I promise to love you until my dying breath." He kissed her upturned nose.

Edie released a long sigh and tried to relax against him.

"Something else is on your mind. Out with it."

"Oh," she said disconsolately. "It's nothing."

"It sure doesn't sound like nothing."

She hesitated a moment, kissed his firm chest, and then tilted her head back so that she met his gaze in the dimly lit room. "Did you talk to Matthew today?"

It was Seth's turn to sigh wearily. "Yeah, I guess you can say that."

"I take it you ran into the same brick wall I did with Chanté?"

"Unfortunately." He rolled onto his back, but kept Edie locked in his arm. "I think they're worse off than I originally thought."

"What do you mean?"

Seth relayed his suspicions about Matt's potentially straying eye and waited for the eruptions he knew that would follow. Edie and Chanté were best friends, after all. Jumping to her girl's defense was only natural.

But she said nothing.

In a way, the quiet was more unsettling than any explosion.

"Baby?"

"Do you think he'll have an affair?"

Seth drew in a deep breath while he replayed what he'd seen in Matt's dressing room and what he knew of his friend's character. He wanted to say "no, absolutely not," but something kept the words from falling from his lips.

Edie sat up. When their eyes met again, Seth read the sadness she felt for her friend. It had nothing to do with book sales or public image.

"We have to try harder," she whispered. "Everyone knows they're soul mates."

"That doesn't mean anything, if they don't know they're soul mates," he reasoned, caressing her arm. "We can lead deer to water, but we can't make them drink."

With a slow nod, she turned toward the window. As she gazed out at the full moon, Seth watched as a smile crept across her face.

"We're going to have to do more than just lead them to the water," she said.

Seth frowned, lost on her meaning.

Edie faced him again. "We're going to have to throw them in."

Chapter 6

Somewhere around two a.m., Matthew began to worry. Would this be the night Chanté decided not to come home? He held his breath as his eyes scanned the dimly lit property. For the last five months he tried to prepare himself for such an occasion, but at this moment he realized he could never truly be prepared for that.

Day after day, he taught and counseled couples on how to rebuild a broken marriage, but he was absolutely clueless on how to fix his own. The sudden beam of a car's headlights piercing the night made Matthew's shoulders deflate with relief.

His marriage would see another day. Break out the champagne.

Matthew moved away from the window and returned to the sofa. He opened his laptop and spread out a folder of paperwork around him. When the door opened, his heartbeat sped up while he questioned if his wife would buy his "working late" act.

The door closed and he heard the locks engage. Soon their nightly script of light bantering would ensue.

Juvenile—yes. Necessary—absolutely.

However, at the sound of Chanté's heels clicking up the stairs, Matthew realized there was an unexpected change in the script. He removed the computer from his lap and rushed to the living room's archway.

"I'm glad to see that you remembered our address," he quipped, crossing his arms. He mentally berated himself for saying the words with blatant concern. He was supposed to sound aloof and nonchalant.

Chanté stopped halfway up the stairs and turned to face him. "Can we not do this tonight? I'm really tired."

Matthew moved from the archway, instantly concerned about the overwhelming sadness in her eyes and her slumped posture.

"Is there…?" He stopped himself at her sudden flash of anger.

"I think you've done enough, don't you?"

He had no response for the soft reprimand. All he could do was watch her turn and climb the rest of her stairs. Exactly one minute later, her high scream filled the entire house.

Matt's heart leaped into the center of his chest as he flew up the stairs. When he rounded the corner to Chanté's room, he quickly skidded to a stop while his eyes grew wide as silver dollars.

The entire room looked as if a tornado had hit. Curtains were pulled from their rods, paper, cotton and goose feathers were spawned across the floor—along with most of the bedding.

"What the hell happened in here?" Matthew asked, though the moment the question was out of his mouth, he suspected the answer.

Chanté rounded on him with fire in her eyes. "You know damn well what happened. You did this!" She stalked toward him.

Raising his hands in surrender, he took a retreating step. "Wait, it's not what you think."

A low growl caught their attention and Chanté slowly turned toward her walk-in closet.

Buddy trotted out, growling and shaking his head with a leather pump clenched between his teeth.

"What in the hell?" Chanté screeched.

"Buddy, no." Matthew raced into the room and knelt to rescue the prized possession. "Give me that. How did you get out of my room?"

"Buddy?" his wife snapped. "This mongrel belongs to you?"

Matthew pried the shoe out of the dog's mouth, but then groaned at the numerous teeth marks around the heel.

Chanté approached with her fist jabbed into her hips.

He glanced up. "Uh, looks like we were a little too late."

"Uh, you think?" She snatched the shoe from his hand. "These are Weitzman pumps. Do you know what I had to do to track these down?"

He quickly scooped the dog into his arms before his wife did something rash. As a matter of fact, he realized that he better stand up if he wanted to keep his own teeth. "Chanté, calm down. This was an accident."

"An accident? You expect me to believe that? What the hell is a dog doing in this house in the first place? You know I don't like dogs."

"Well, I do. And I think it's high time I had one. I need something around here to be happy when I come home."

She sucked in an indignant breath. "And who is going to take care of him?"

"I'll take care of him!"

Chanté swept out an arm to indicate her bedroom. "Does this look like you're taking care of him?"

"He must have gotten out of his crate."

"Did you come to that conclusion all by yourself, Dr. Valentine?"

"It was an accident. It won't happen again."

Rage trembled through Chanté's body like a bolt of lightning. "Get out!" she seethed through her clenched teeth.

"Chanté…"

Pivoting on her heel, she marched toward the door and held it open. "I said, get out."

Realizing that she wasn't going to listen to reason, Matthew waltzed out. He'd barely crossed the threshold when the door slammed behind him.

Matthew stood still for a long moment, reviewing what had just happened.

Just apologize. Seth's advice rang in Matt's ear and reverberated through every cell of his body.

But apologize for what? Okay, maybe he could start with the car and the damage the dog did to her room—or even his callous remarks on national television. But all of that transpired in the last week. It would hardly cover the past five months.

It's a start.

Matthew turned around and knocked on the door.

Chanté didn't answer.

He drew a deep breath and tried again—this time a little louder. When she didn't answer the second time, he knew he was officially being given the silent treatment.

"I just wanted to say I'm sorry," he murmured to the door.

Buddy lifted his head and delivered a sloppy lick against Matthew's cheek.

"At least you still like me." Turning, Matthew followed the gray duct tape back to his room.

Thinking she heard something, Chanté shut off the shower and waited to see if she'd hear it again. After a minute, she shivered from the cool chill of the bathroom and turned the hot water back on. The steady, warm pulse of the water did a considerable job of easing the tension from her body.

However, she fully intended to make herself a

hard drink once she climbed out of the shower—maybe even two.

As she lathered and rinsed, lathered and rinsed, she churned an inventory of Matthew's prized possessions over in her mind. Which item would pack the most wallop and which one would hit below the belt?

How long are you going to keep this up?

The question threw her, mainly because she didn't have an answer. This tit-for-tat game they played was taking on a life of its own, and in a weird way, it fed something in her—in Matthew, too, if she wasn't mistaken.

She shut off the water again and stepped out of the shower. Wrapping the towel around her body, she traipsed back into the adjoining bedroom. She stripped everything off the bed, and then put on fresh linens before she crawled on top.

Sighing, she stared up at the ceiling and laughed. She laughed so hard and so long, the voice inside her head questioned her sanity.

Sitting up, she took a long look around her gilded cage—albeit a trashed cage—and felt an incredible loneliness. It hadn't always felt this way—not when Matthew used to lie beside her. Chanté groaned. Why did her heart constantly flip-flop where Matthew was concerned?

She loved him. She hated him. She loved him. She loved him.

"Aw, hell. Maybe Edie was right. Maybe we do need help." After all, it had been easy to fall in love with Matthew, though many of her friends thought they were oil and water from the start.

Growing up, she hadn't known any affluent black families—not in a small Texan town like Karankawa. She was charmed by everything from the way he talked to the way he walked. She was in awe of his intelligence, captivated by his sophistication and seduced by his good looks.

While wallowing in a moment of honesty, she realized he still had those qualities. Maybe she was the one who'd changed. Maybe if her body had given them a child, she wouldn't be so bitter.

She stretched out across the bed, hoping to fill the empty spaces—but it didn't work. Chanté closed her eyes and struggled to remember all of their firsts. The first time he took her into his arms. Their first kiss. The first time they made love. After a while, the memories flooded her senses.

The first time they were together they'd lain on a bed of rose petals. Roses were her favorite flowers. That night, she thought she'd die from the sheer joy of their consummation. The tenderness of his probing and inquisitive hands. He was masterful in figuring out all her hot spots.

She remembered his mouth tasting like a fusion of heaven and sin. One minute, she was his precious angel and in the next, his little devil. Back then, Matthew kept a beautifully groomed goatee and her sensitive skin always quivered beneath its light tickle.

Lost in the memories, Chanté unwrapped the towel from her baby-oiled body and fanned her fingers across her chest. Oh, what she wouldn't give to travel back in time and experience that night again. Love seemed so effortless and happiness was always just a kiss away.

Nothing is stopping you from going to him now.

Her eyes snapped open. For a second her eyes darted around to see if someone else had actually made the comment. When she realized she was still alone, she sighed in relief.

But the bud of her femininity began to ache for fulfillment.

"I could go," she whispered, warming to the idea. Heck, who said that she had to apologize in order to get laid? Hell, she didn't even have to talk.

Chanté sucked in her bottom lip and nibbled for a little while. *There's the danger of Matthew thinking that sex would be some sort of peace offering.*

The ache between her legs intensified.

Then again, I could correct him in the morning. Chanté liked that idea and bounded off the bed, in search of the perfect negligee to seduce her husband.

Chapter 7

After a half bottle of Jack Daniels, Matthew dreamed of his wife's creamy thighs, firm breasts and perfect apple bottom. He tossed and turned and even smacked his lips while remembering her distinctive taste. The wanting, aching and longing had stripped him of his sanity.

No matter how many times he tried to think or concentrate on something else, Chanté's teasing body would crystallize in his mind. If he thought about work, Chanté would materialize as a naked cue-card girl. When writing material for his next book, Chanté would be the naked girl on his Internet pop-up, asking him if he wanted to see her in action.

It was maddening…and a complete turn-on.

In need of relief, Matthew grabbed hold of his erection and tried to assuage the ache. Even at this desperate hour, his hand was a lousy substitute.

You could always go back and knock on the door again.

Matthew's hand stilled. The thought had possibilities. But then he remembered how Chanté had turned him down the other night and how she closed the door in his face tonight. How many times could he face her rejection?

Knock. Knock.

Matthew remained frozen in the bed with his erection still throbbing in his hand.

Knock. Knock.

Buddy barked from his crate.

"Yes?" he asked sluggishly.

Instead of an answer, he listened as the doorknob turned and the heavy door creaked open. Pushing himself up, he wasn't quite sure what to expect—an intruder, his wife, or an intruder impersonating his wife.

He waited until the curvaceous figure illuminated under the silvery moonlight. Even then he wasn't sure he believed what he was seeing or if his old buddy Jack now had him hallucinating.

"Chanté?"

She glided toward the bed and pressed a slender finger against his lips. It didn't take a rocket scientist to catch her meaning—and he was only too willing to oblige.

Damn it, it's been five months.

Wait, his brain screamed. *Something wasn't right.* Matt eyed her suspiciously. "Is this a trick?"

Again, she didn't answer. Just gave him a slight shake of her head.

Matthew weighed whether to believe her. Then again, if this was a hallucination, what harm was there in having a little fun?

A bright smile bloomed across Matthew's face and glowed in the moonlight. "Hey, baby. You finally decided to come pay Big Daddy a visit?"

Chanté frowned. "Have you been drinking?"

"Maybe. Maybe not. There's no law against a man drinking in the privacy of his own home, is there?"

"Never mind. This was a mistake." She turned.

Matthew hopped out of bed and clutched her arm. "Don't go, baby. You know we've both been waiting for this for a long time," he slurred.

She hesitated, giving Matthew all the confirmation he needed.

"Why don't you give me a big, fat juicy kiss to seal the deal?"

Eager, both Chanté and Matthew leaned forward, only to bang their foreheads together.

"Ouch."

"Oh. Sorry about that." Matt fluttered a nervous smile before trying again. This time, their lips connected and their bodies sagged with relief.

However, when Matt leaned her back onto the bed, he'd forgotten about his laptop and piles of paper occupying the other side.

"Ow, ouch." Chanté shoved him off.

"Oh, just a minute." Matt pitched everything, including the laptop, over the side of the bed. "See? All gone." He flashed another toothy smile and clumsily reached for her again.

Buddy barked.

"Shh. Buddy, be quiet," Matthew warned. "You'll scare my dream girl away."

Chanté hesitated.

"Don't worry, no more surprises," he assured, patting the empty bed for emphasis.

After another beat of hesitation, Chanté decided to give it another try. She glided effortlessly into his arms and imagined herself cast into her own romance novel. But everything didn't play out quite the way she'd hope.

Matthew grabbed for her like a starved man before an all-you-can-eat buffet. He fumbled and cursed while he tried to pry her out of her lingerie.

"Here, let me do it," she offered before he had a chance to destroy one more thing of hers. Three snaps later, she chiseled on another smile and then lay back on the bed in all her naked glory.

That was when the real pawing began.

Matt's once tender and caressing hands were now rough and forceful. Lips that once gave loving worship to her sensitive nipples now seemed determined to chew the damn things off.

"Easy. Easy," she coached, wanting him to slow down and enjoy the ride. Instead, her husband skipped foreplay and went straight for the main attraction.

He entered with one mighty thrust and nearly split her in two.

What the hell?

Chanté gripped his bulging biceps and tried to hold on during the ride. However, she was nearly rendered senseless several times as her head was rammed into the headboard. Meanwhile, Buddy continued to bark his head off. This was like nothing she'd ever experienced before.

"Shh, Buddy. Shh, Buddy," Matthew hissed in between his "Oh, Gods." His hips hammered away while his eyes damn near rolled to the back of his head.

Chanté watched in resolute boredom until

Matthew stiffened with one last thrust, and then collapsed in a sweaty heap.

Is that it?

"Oh, baby. I missed you so much." Matthew panted and peppered sloppy kisses across her face and eyes.

"Uhm." She searched for the right words. "Matt?"

"Hmm?"

"I, uh, didn't…well, you know."

Matt lifted his head and stared down at her. "You didn't?"

Chanté shook her head. *Not even close.*

"I, uh, I'm so—well, I guess, I did get a little carried away. It being a while and all." He absently wiped the sweat from his brow.

She nodded in feigned understanding. "That's all right. You can try again."

"Yeah, yeah." He smiled and wiggled his hips.

To Chanté's dismay, she noted Matt Jr. wasn't exactly standing at full salute.

"Just give me a minute to…catch my breath," Matthew panted.

Chanté's brows furrowed, but she had no choice but to bob her head in agreement and wait for her husband to catch his second wind.

Two minutes later, Matthew was fast asleep.

At breakfast the next morning, Seth decided it was time he dusted off his culinary skills to make his wife breakfast in bed. Unfortunately, his specialty was cold cereal.

"Oh, honey." Edie smiled brightly when he appeared at their bedroom doorway with her breakfast tray in hand. "You shouldn't have."

Seth beamed proudly as if he'd prepared a five-course meal. "My baby deserves the best."

"Special K, huh?"

"Special K with strawberries."

"Then bring it on!" Edie set aside the pamphlets in her lap and punched up her pillows before her husband delivered her meal.

"What are these?" he asked, picking up one of the pamphlets.

"Some brochures I picked up yesterday before my talk with Chanté."

Seth frowned as he opened one and then another. "Sex therapy? I thought the idea was to get them to see a real counselor?"

"They're real." Edie snatched one of the brochures back. "I've heard some great things about these places."

"Where? On one of those women's talk shows?"

Edie poked out her bottom lip as she shrugged her shoulders. "What if I did? A reference is a reference."

"Okay, this job just went from difficult to impossible." Seth laughed. "Sex isn't the problem. Their ability to stay away from sharp objects is."

"Are you sure about that?" she asked, scooping out her first spoonful of cereal.

"No," he acquiesced. "It's not the sort of thing we talk about."

"Well, what do you talk about?"

"His lack of sex. Five months and counting." Seth shook his head with great sympathy. "I don't care what anyone says, that's cruel and unusual punishment. No wonder he's demolishing cars."

"I hear you." She chomped away for a moment while her gaze returned to the pamphlets.

"Actually, I really think I'm on to something here. Last week when Chanté stormed over here about the Letterman incident, she said that Matthew *used* to be great in bed."

"What the hell? Do you two give each other blow-by-blow recaps?"

"Don't worry, sweetie. You're still a ten in my book."

Seth straightened his shoulders as his chest swelled from the compliment. "Ten is easy when I have an eleven in my arms."

For that, he was rewarded with a kiss.

"So you think this sex therapy will work?"

"It certainly can't hurt."

"Not unless there's a chainsaw on the premises."
Edie chuckled.

"Any idea how we're going to get them to one of these places?" Seth asked.

"Yes. We lie."

Chapter 8

Chanté was beyond pissed.

No car. No foreplay. No orgasm. Enough was enough.

She slammed the kitchen cabinets as she made coffee, took her morning pills, and slaved over the hot stove. Every time she thought about last night's lousy performance, she broke a glass, a cup or a dish. How and when did Matt become so selfish and so clueless in bed?

Not only had he fallen asleep, he snored loud enough to wake the dead.

Crash!

Another plate bit the dust.

"Good morning."

Chanté's gaze snapped to her husband as he entered the kitchen, and for a brief moment she weighed the consequences of smashing his head in with a frying pan.

The temptation nearly won out—especially since the bastard had the audacity to be in a cheerful mood.

"What smells so good?" he asked, with a beaming smile.

"Breakfast," she answered with an overdose of saccharine. "Hungry?"

Suspicion glimmered in Matt's eyes. "You're cooking me breakfast?"

"It's not unusual for a wife to cook for her husband."

Matthew's brows shot up.

"Why don't you just take a seat at the table? The food will be right out."

Matt didn't move. Instead, he studied the angles of her plastic smile. "Uh…about last night," he began. "Did we…you didn't come to my room last night, did you?"

The jerk doesn't even remember! Chanté crossed her arms and weighed her options. "Only in your dreams," she lied bitterly.

"Oh, I didn't think so." He shook his head and gave an awkward laugh. "I knew I had a few too many."

Chanté glared and contemplated the frying pan again. "Breakfast will be out in a minute."

He hesitated again.

"Go on now. I'll be out there in a second."

Finally, he gave her a slight nod and then turned in the direction of the dining room.

I'll fix you breakfast all right. One you'll never forget.

Matt knew he was in trouble. Why on earth would Chanté fix him breakfast after what Buddy did to her room? The way he saw it, he still had options. He could either run from the house screaming like a banshee, put in a precall to 9-1-1, or drop to his knees and beg for mercy.

The first option had potential.

"Breakfast is ready," Chanté sang, carrying plates to the table.

Too late. Matthew swallowed a lump in his throat while his brain threatened to short-circuit with trying to come up with an excuse to miss breakfast.

"Uh, Chanté." He followed his wife to the table.

"Yes, dear?"

Dear? "You know, I'm not all that hungry," he said with a nervous smile. However, the sight of fluffy scrambled eggs, crisp bacon and golden-brown biscuits made his stomach roar at the lie.

Chanté lifted an inquisitive brow.

"Maybe I am a little hungry."

Chanté smiled and pulled out a chair. "Sit."

Matt hesitated. His fear accelerated at the sight of her lips sliding wider.

"Come on." She patted the back of the chair. "You're not afraid of me, are you?"

How could he back down from a challenge like that? "Of course not." He walked over to her, searched her eyes for any telltale signs and then slowly eased into the offered chair.

"There. See?" She patted his shoulders. "That wasn't so bad, was it?"

The corner of Matthew's lips quivered and then he glanced down at the meal before him. Everything looked good—perhaps too good.

Chanté hummed a merry tune like a Disney princess as she walked to the other side of the table to take her seat. "Dig in," she said.

Matt glanced around. "You know, I think I'd like some orange juice," he announced, scooting back his chair. "Can I get you any?"

"I'll get it." She jumped up from her chair and nearly raced out of the room. "You sit there and eat."

When she disappeared around the corner, he reached across the table and switched the plates. A second later his wife rushed back into the room carrying two glasses of orange juice. "Here you go."

"Thank you, honey."

Her smile thinned at the endearment and Matthew grew suspicious of the drink she handed him as well. Mercifully, Buddy chose that moment to waddle into the room.

"What in the hell is he doing in here?" Chanté snapped and jumped up from the table.

"Hey, little Buddy." Matt scooped up the dog. "How do you keep getting out of your crate?"

"Get him out of here!" Chanté screeched.

Matthew cradled the dog against his body. "All right. Calm down. Don't have a conniption fit. I'll go put him back in his crate."

"Apparently he needs a stronger crate. Tie him up somewhere outside."

Buddy barked.

Chanté stuck her tongue out at the dog.

"Now is that mature?" Matthew asked.

"After what he did to my bedroom, he's lucky we're not having him for breakfast."

Buddy whimpered and snuggled against his owner.

Unmoved, Chanté stomped her foot. "Outside."

"Come on, Buddy. Let's see if Roger can get you situated somewhere." Matthew rose from his chair and marched out, all the while cooing and apologizing to the dog for his wife's behavior.

Chanté leaned across the table and craned her neck to see if the coast was clear and then quickly switched the breakfast plates back.

Minutes later, her husband returned with a pinch of annoyance in his expression. The emotion vanished when he discovered his wife had already started eating her meal. He eased into his chair and watched her expression.

Chanté stopped chewing and frowned.

"Is something wrong, honey?" Matthew picked up his fork.

"No." She smiled but it faltered. "Everything is…fine."

He returned the smile when she placed a hand over her stomach. "Good." He dove into his food triumphantly and moaned aloud to emphasize how wonderful everything tasted. "You know, honey. I think this is the best breakfast I've had in a long time."

"Glad you enjoy it." Grimacing, she cupped a hand over her mouth. "Excuse me." She bounded out her chair and raced out of the room.

Matt shoved another forkful of food into his mouth while chuckling to himself. *You have to get up pretty early in the morning to pull one over on me.*

In the half bathroom on the bottom floor, Chanté was doubled over with laughter.

The studio audience for *The Love Doctor* show grew restless waiting for their host to take the stage. The warm-up team had long run out of jokes and prizes to hand out and the camera crew and stagehands were growing bored.

"Where is he?" Trish from the sound department inquired. "Production is going to run over."

"Love Doctor! Love Doctor!" the crowd chanted.

"We'd better do something or we're going to have a studio of emotionally imbalanced women storm the stage," Trish warned.

"Love Doctor! Love Doctor!"

"I'll go check his dressing room," Cookie volunteered cheerfully and sashayed off.

Matthew wasn't feeling too good. In fact, he was feeling downright miserable—and he knew why.

"I'm never going to forgive her for this," he vowed, exiting his private bathroom. Despite his black mood, he finally managed to pull himself together and leave his dressing room.

"There you are!" Cookie approached, wearing a wide smile. "Everyone is waiting for you." Studying his face, the intern frowned. "Are you all right? You don't look so well."

"Fine." Matthew flashed a smile but proceeded to take tiny steps toward the stage. "Never better." He stopped and closed his eyes as another wave of nausea threatened to send him back to the toilet.

Cookie stopped, fearful that whatever he had was contagious.

After a few seconds, Matthew sighed in relief when his stomach settled and he continued his slow journey to the stage.

"Love Doctor! Love Doctor!" the crowd chanted.

"There he is!" a spectator shouted from the crowd, and the studio thundered with applause.

Matthew smiled, waved and hit his mark in front of the cameras. However, the moment he opened his mouth his stomach dropped to his knees and his nausea was no longer ripples but huge tidal waves.

"Hello, everyone," he greeted, struggling to remain professional. Yet, the moment the stage lights turned up, he literally felt beads of sweat pop up along his forehead. "Thanks for coming…and good night." Matthew turned and bolted off the stage, praying that he would make it back to his private bathroom.

"What type of conference is this again?" Chanté asked Edie for the third time as they perused the shoe aisles. "And why do both Matt and I have to attend?"

"It's a relationship conference and you're going because it's an excellent promotional opportunity. A lot of press is covering this thing so you and Matt need to be on your best behavior."

Chanté sighed and rolled her eyes. "I don't know, Edie. I sort of need a break from Matthew—especially after last night's fiasco. I wanted to kill that damn dog…and him." She hesitated and then cast a sidelong glance over at her friend.

"What?"

Chanté debated on whether she should tell everything that had happened. "I went to Matthew's bedroom last night."

Edie's eyes lit up. "You did? Well, good for you!" She gave her a strong hug and noticed Chanté's lack of response. "Not good?"

"I'd rather have played Scrabble."

Edie grimaced.

"No kissing. No foreplay. No nothing," Chanté whispered angrily. "He just tossed me back onto the bed, pumped like an Olympic record was on the line…and then rolled over and went to sleep."

"Ouch."

"Damn right. I wanted to kill him." She

stopped there, not confessing to tampering with Matthew's breakfast. No need to paint herself in a bad light. "I just don't get it," Chanté complained. "He wasn't always like this. I remember a time— Ooh, girl. The earth moved, angels flew down from heaven and I thought I'd need physical therapy in order to walk again. Now? It's wham-bam-thank-you-ma'am and, by the way, where is the baby?"

Edie fell silent as she cocked her head in sympathy.

"I used to think we were just in some kind of rut. You know, stress from the jobs, the pressure to try and beat my biological clock. Before I knew it, long lovemaking sessions were downgraded to quickies and we've been stuck in that same gear ever since."

"I'm sorry." Edie draped an arm around her friend's shoulders. Now she was convinced more than ever that she was doing the right thing in tricking Chanté and Matthew into sex therapy. "Look, go to this conference. When you get back, I'll make sure you get a break. I'll talk to Julia in the publicity department and arrange a book tour for you. That'll keep you out of the house for a little while."

"True." Chanté sighed, but then perked up. "Ooh. These are nice." She picked up a pair of leather pumps.

"Don't you already have a pair like that?"

"No. It doesn't have this cute little buckle on the side. I'm going to try them on."

Edie just shook her head as she followed her friend to a nearby chair where she asked a saleswoman for the correct size. "No offense, but how many shoes can one woman own?"

"Hey, when I was growing up, I never owned more than two pairs of shoes at a time."

"And now you have a whole department store in your closet."

"All right, I admit it. I love shoes. Sue me."

Edie continued to shake her head. "So what do you say? Will you do the conference?"

"Separate hotel rooms?"

"C'mon. How will that look at a relationship conference?"

"Like we're trying to preserve our sanity."

"Chanté."

"All right. All right." She held up her hands.

"You'll do it?" Her editor perked up.

Chanté drew a deep breath and tried to figure out just how long she and Matthew could share a hotel room without a homicide detective showing up.

"Please?" Edie folded her hands in mock prayer.

"All right. I'll do it," she huffed. "Just make sure the room is stocked with enough alcohol to dull my pain."

Edie smiled smugly behind Chanté's back. *One down, one to go.*

Chapter 9

"I'm not going anywhere with that psycho!" Matthew spat to Seth and then ducked his head back over the toilet bowl. "If you haven't noticed, she damn near tried to kill me this morning."

"Am I to believe that you did nothing to provoke her attempted murder this time?"

"No," he lied, coming up for air again. "Well…not exactly."

"Uh-huh." Seth finished wringing cold water from a face towel and then tossed it to his client.

"What exactly did you do? It wouldn't happen to have involved a four-legged friend I told you not to take home?"

Matthew placed the towel over his face, in part to cool his forehead and in part to hide his guilt while he reviewed last night's major disasters...and one mind-blowing sex dream.

"If it's taking you that long to answer the question, I don't think I want to know what happened."

"That's probably best." He paused and then added, "I think my, uh, streak ended last night."

Seth's eyebrows rose in surprise, but then quickly crash-landed. "You think? I take it since the porcelain god is your best friend today that it didn't go too well?"

"Horrible," Matthew groaned. "I was drunk and it had been so long...I grew too excited...and was a little quick on the trigger." He glanced up at Seth. "And that's not the worst part."

"You didn't."

He nodded. "I did. I fell asleep...and then this morning I wasn't sure if I'd dreamed the whole thing. When I asked Chanté about it, she said that it never happened, but I don't know."

It was Seth's turn to groan.

"I didn't mean for it to happen," Matthew said defensively. "It just did. And then this morning when she was cooking breakfast I started to apologize…and I couldn't quite get the words out. Me! King of the talk shows couldn't find the words to apologize to my wife. How pathetic is that?"

"No wonder she tried to kill you."

"Nothing excuses that."

"And what excuse is there for taking a chain-saw to someone's car?"

"Hey! Just whose side are you on?"

"No one's side since you're both crazy as hell." Seth folded his arms as he leaned back against the sink. "C'mon, Matt. About this conference—it's going to be great for you publicly. A few of the other top relationship gurus are going to be there."

"Dr. Phil?"

"If I'm not mistaken," Seth lied smoothly. "It's just for a couple of days. Surely you and Chanté can put your differences aside for a couple of days to pose as the perfect couple?"

Matthew groaned his doubt, especially since his mind was already churning for his next payback for being damn near poisoned. "I don't know, Seth. I think what we need is a vacation from one another. Maybe you can set me up with a book tour or something. Get me out of the house before I make America's Most Wanted list."

"All right. You do this conference and when you get back, I'll get you your tour."

After hosting another long night of *The Open Heart Forum*, Chanté broke her promise and issued Thad yet another rain check. Mostly, she didn't feel like hosting another pity party. What good would it do?

"Piss or get off the pot." How many women had she told that to over the years? If you're not happy, why stick around?

"And the hypocrisy award goes to…me."

At two a.m., she turned the rental car into the driveway, but sat behind the wheel long after she shut off the engine. To be honest, she was afraid to go inside. Matthew was not likely to let a little thing like spiking his food go unavenged. Of course it was harmless—at most he was nauseous for a couple of hours—at worst he spent the day hugging the toilet.

Like always—she had options. Grab a hotel room for the night, sleep in the car or brave out Matthew's next chess move. In the end, her curiosity was too strong to back down.

Opening the front door, Chanté peered cautiously inside. The first clue that something was up was that all the lights in the house were turned off. Matthew was giving the appearance that he hadn't waited up for her.

She didn't buy it for a minute.

Chanté inched across the threshold with bated breath and her ears strained to catch the slightest sound. Closing the door, she effectively stamped out the only light resource she had. She knew the layout of the house by heart and rushed across the foyer to take the stairs two at a time. If she could just make it to her bedroom, she'd be safe.

But once in her bedroom, she discovered Matthew's revenge.

The scream she released was more bloodcurdling than all the horror movie scream queens put together. There, strung from the ceiling like party favors, were hundreds of her precious shoes: Prada, Gucci, Ferragamos and even her $14,000 Manolo Blahnik alligator boots, with all their heels severed.

Her shoes. Her babies.

She screamed until she realized this was not a dream or, better yet, a nightmare. "I'm going to kill him," she seethed. Glancing around, Chanté looked for a weapon—any weapon.

"Payback is a bitch," Matthew drawled from behind.

She spun around and launched at him.

Matthew never imagined his wife could move so quickly. Before he could think to block the attack she was already on him like white on rice. After she landed a few blows upside his head, he lost his balance and toppled onto the floor where they rolled around like seasoned wrestlers.

"I hate you! I hate you!" Chanté shouted at the top of her lungs. "How could you do such a thing?"

Because you tried to kill me, he tried to say, but the moment he opened his mouth, she socked him in it.

"Chanté, it's never okay to hit," he managed to scowl.

"Screw you!"

They continued to grapple. She took the top position, then it was his turn, and then her turn again.

"Goddamn it, Matthew. You've gone too far this time."

"Me?" he thundered incredulously. "I could have ended up in the hospital over that stunt you pulled this morning."

"If only I could be so lucky," she snapped.

The rush of small padded paws rushed across the hardwood floor and Chanté glanced up in time to see the short squat bulldog barreling and barking toward her. She jumped just as Matthew shoved and flew back, and smacked her head with a loud thump on the corner of the bedroom's doorframe.

"Chanté!" Matthew sat up. "Are you all right?"

"Oww." She sucked in a deep breath and rubbed at the instant knot on the back of her head. "That hurt." As Buddy continued to bark at full volume, Chanté had an evil image of skewering the dog and roasting him over an open pit.

"Shut him up!"

Matthew scooped Buddy up and jogged him back to his room. By the time he returned, Chanté managed to pull herself up off the floor and limp to the bed.

"Are you all right?" he asked again.

"Of course." She didn't attempt to look in his direction. "Don't I look all right?"

Matthew crossed the room to her bed. "Mind if I take a look?"

His gruff baritone held a warmth she recognized from years long past and she was surprised by a sudden flutter in the pit of her stomach. She jumped when his hand gently touched the back of her head.

"Be still. I promise I won't hurt you…this time."

Why in the hell did she smile? Had he finally knocked the rest of her marbles loose?

Tilting her head, Chanté's sanity was again called into question when her husband's fingers combed through her hair and her heartbeat quickened.

It had to be a trick of the mind when time crawled at a snail's pace during her examination. Sitting still and trying not to make any additional contact, she noticed for the first time his change in cologne. For years his signature scent was the sandalwood-based Hugo by Hugo Boss. She had been the one to introduce the fragrance to him as a Christmas gift back in '96. He loved it because she loved it and he'd worn it ever since.

Now this tangy scent reeked as being a gift from another woman. Chanté sucked in a breath from the sudden conclusion and she pulled away.

Misinterpreting her reaction, Matthew held up his hands and backed away. "Looks like you'll live."

Chanté eyed him suspiciously, looking to see if there were any other clues that hinted that there was another woman in the picture. She found none, but once the thought escaped Pandora's box, she couldn't force it back inside.

"I want a divorce," she said in a croaked whisper.

Matthew sighed.

"I mean it this time," she added as tears gathered in her eyes. "We can't keep living this way." Standing from the bed, her head bumped against a pair of Jimmy Choos. "It's time we let go."

Her words skillfully carved Matthew's heart out of his chest. It was probably the millionth time she'd asked for a divorce and probably the first time he knew that she meant it.

And it was the first time he was truly scared.

"We'll talk about it in the morning," he said, almost failing to get the words out of his constricting throat.

"I'm not going to change my mind," she informed him softly. Her eyes swam in a pool of tears. "The only reason we're still together is because of our careers. How pathetic is that?"

Chanté reached up and began pulling the shoes down from the ceiling. Fat tears rolled like boulders down her face.

"I went too far—"

"We both did," she said sadly. "I, uh, did promise Edie we would attend some big conference coming up."

"Yeah. Seth asked me about it today."

"I think I can manage one last happy face for the public. How about you?"

"Piece of cake."

She nodded and wiped her face dry. "When we return, I'm seeing my lawyer."

Matthew clenched his jaw at the sound of the final nail being hammered into their marriage's coffin and turned to leave before his tears fell.

Chapter 10

For three days, the Valentines' household had transformed into a multimillion-dollar tomb. Even Buddy seemed to take on his owner's melancholy and gave up barking.

At seeing the short, stout mongrel following her to the kitchen, Chanté couldn't bring herself to get angry with him for having escaped his crate again. Especially not with him looking up at her the way he did. His wide-eyed stare seemed to urge her to tell him her problems.

More than once, she found herself doing just that—usually when she found herself filling his dog bowl with kibble.

"I just don't know if I can handle four days pretending to be happy when I'm not," she told Buddy. "And I don't know what I'm going to say when the divorce becomes public."

Buddy whined as he put his head down on the cold kitchen floor.

"I know," she whispered, retrieving a box of cereal. "I still can't believe it's over." She filled a glass with water, took her morning pills and then finished fixing her breakfast. She settled on a stool at the breakfast bar. In her head, she scrolled through a list of questions she usually asked her callers who were at the end of a relationship.

Have you exhausted all avenues for reconciliation?

Before she lied to herself, Edie's voice floated around her head. *Maybe you and Matt should seek counseling.*

Like before, she scoffed at the idea, but then looking around her kitchen and imagining what it would truly be like when Matthew moved out, she reconsidered.

The moment her morning meeting with the marketing department was over, Edie raced back to her cluttered office ready to dive into a stack of unread manuscripts, but instead was surprised to see her handsome husband waiting for her.

"Baby, what are you doing here?" She eased into his arms and delivered a quick smooch against his smooth-shaved skin.

"Came to see if I could take my favorite girl to lunch…and to see if you have those fake itineraries printed up. I'm running by the studio this afternoon and I promised Matthew I'd bring them to him."

"Got them right here on my desk." She moved to her in-box and then handed him a glossy folder.

"The Marriage Quest conference," he read aloud. "Catchy."

"Why, thank you." Edie's smile beamed as she rocked on her heels. "I can't take all the credit. Julia in Publicity helped."

"The Tree of Life Spa and Resort," he continued reading. "Sounds interesting."

"Oh, it is. The tree of life is a part of the map of the seven chakras."

"The what?"

"Chakras. They are energy centers that represent the dynamic flow of cosmic energy within the human body."

"Uh-huh." He snapped the folder closed. "Fascinating."

"It is," Edie went on. "You know, I was thinking—maybe we should go with Chanté and Matthew."

"Why? There's nothing wrong with our sex life." Seth stepped back and folded his arms. "Is there?"

"No. No. Of course not." She slyly opened his arms and eased back into his embrace. "But I thought it would be fun for us to try out new things. Plus, we'll probably need to keep an eye out on Matthew and Chanté. We have to stop them from bolting when they discover they've been tricked."

"What are we supposed to do—tackle them?"

"Love is a contact sport." She laughed at her own joke.

Seth failed to see the humor.

"C'mon. We should really be there for them."

Never being able to resist his wife's pleading brown eyes, Seth gave in with a sigh. "All right. All right. I'll clear my schedule."

"Good. I already bought our tickets."

"Of course you did."

Matthew spent another day cruising on autopilot. He listened with great apathy to his guests' problems, doled out his earnest opinions and advice, and then smiled and laughed with his staff once they wrapped taping.

In the coming week, the network would broadcast repeat programming while he attended his last conference with his wife. A part of him knew that he should at least give his producers a heads-up about the pending divorce, but the other part of him still hadn't come to terms with it.

That was silly, considering their wild fights

and inexcusable behavior. Deep down, he never thought she would go through with it. She was his yin to his yang. If she got crazy, he went crazy, too.

But leave?

"I should have followed Seth's advice and just apologized," he mumbled to the vanity mirror inside his dressing room.

"I'm sorry. Did you say something?" Cookie asked, handing him his coffee.

"No. No. I was just…talking to myself." He smiled blandly and dropped his gaze to the steaming black liquid in his favorite *Open Heart Forum* coffee mug.

"Oh." Cookie clasped her hands behind her back and thrust her surgically-enhanced bosom high into the air. "Well, is there anything else I can do for you?"

"No. I think that's all. Thank you." He sipped from his cup and prepared to dive back into his desolate thoughts.

"Are you sure?" The young girl stepped forward and purposely rubbed her breasts against his arm.

"Can't you think of anything else you might need?"

Surprised, Matthew instinctively pulled his arm away and repositioned himself in his chair to avoid physical contact. Yes, she was a beauty by any man's standards and there was no misinterpreting the open invitation written in her eyes, but he was a married man and…

His thoughts froze. He wasn't going to be a married man much longer. His war against his advancing depression ended in a crushing defeat.

His marriage was over.

Old man Roger agreed to keep an eye on Buddy for the Valentines. When he showed up to pick the puppy up, he innocently asked, "You guys going to a funeral?"

Matthew handed their luggage to the chauffer and shot a look over at his wife.

As if a director had shouted action, she gave an Oscar-worthy performance by laughing off the question and patting the groundskeeper's arm. "Nothing as serious as that. We're guest speakers for a marriage and relationship conference in New Mexico."

"Ah." He nodded his head, but his eyes darted between the couple.

Matthew thought the man didn't look convinced, but at least he had the decency not to probe further.

"Well, you two have a good time. Don't you worry none about Buddy. I'll take good care of him."

A few minutes later, they headed off to the airport. Within five minutes, the drive already seemed too long. Matthew sat ramrod straight while trying not to glance over at his wife. The few times he caught a glimpse of her, she stared resolutely out the window.

"You know, it's not too late to back out of this," he said, breaking the chilly silence.

Chanté glanced at him, seemingly annoyed that he was speaking to her.

"We could just give them some type of excuse...or tell them the truth."

The way she pressed back into her seat and

carefully folded her arms, Matthew surmised she was tempted by the suggestion. In turn, it felt like another nail being driven into their coffin.

"I promised Edie I would go," she admitted softly. "Might as well go ahead and just get it over with."

"Yeah," he agreed, returning his attention to the scenery sliding past his own window. "Might as well."

Later, the husband and wife team arrived at the airport and stepped out of the limousine with wide toothy smiles. Matthew, being a sort of television celebrity, was more immediately recognized and was approached for autographs.

"Oh, my Lord. It really is you," one woman gushed, covering her heart with both hands. "Oh, I absolutely love your show." She turned her dancing eyes toward Chanté and dug through her large purse. "And I just purchased your book this morning. Will you sign it for me?"

"I'd love to," Chanté returned the woman's infectious smile.

The woman handed over the book and prattled

on. "I was telling my girlfriend the other day about what a beautiful couple you two make."

"Why, thank you," Matthew and Chanté responded like robots.

"Look, it's the Valentines," another woman gasped and then preceded to drag her unimpressed companion toward them. Within seconds it was apparent the woman had a major crush on Matthew.

"Honey, make sure you keep your claws in this one," gushing woman number two whispered loudly to Chanté. "Trust me. They don't make them like him anymore."

A few inches evaporated from Chanté's smile as she cast a sidelong glance at her husband. No question about it, Matthew was indeed a fine specimen. His aura of confidence and warm baritone practically had the women melting all over him.

Her, too, if she wasn't careful.

The Valentines worked their way toward their gate, smiling and giving one another adoring glances.

Sometimes it was forced, sometimes it wasn't.

After settling into their first-class seats, Chanté and Matthew blinked in genuine surprise when Edie and Seth took the seats across the aisle from them.

"What are you two doing here?" Chanté asked with a rush of relief, easing into her bones.

"What do you think?" Edie chided, and then lowered her voice. "We're here to make sure you two don't kill each other."

"Personally, I welcome the protection," Matthew joked, and was rewarded with a sharp elbow jab. "See what I mean?" he added.

"All right, you two. Behave," Seth warned, shaking his head. "Don't make us put you in time-out."

"He/She started it," Chanté and Matthew complained in unison and then gave each other sharp looks.

Seth leaned into his wife's ear. "Still think this is going to work?"

Edie thrust up her chin and gave him a reassuring smile. "Trust me. Once we get to the resort they'll be thanking us."

Chapter 11

"What the hell do you mean there's no conference?" Chanté rounded on her best friend once the group arrived at the front desk of The Tree of Life Spa and Resort. "I have a full itinerary and workshop program—"

"I sort of made those up," Edie admitted and then used her husband as a human shield in case Chanté put her good pinching fingers to use.

"You made them up?" Matthew and Chanté barked.

"Why would you do something like that?" Chanté asked. "Do you know what I had to do to get this time off from the radio station on such short notice?"

"Mr. and Mrs. Valentine?" A calm, gentle female voice spoke from behind them.

Chanté and Matthew turned cautiously toward an elderly white-haired woman who was just shy of five feet tall.

"Hello, I'm Dr. Margaret Gardner. Welcome to The Tree of Life Resort. I can't tell you how excited I was that you two had registered for our Sexuality and Liberation program."

"Come again?" Matthew shot a glare at Seth.

"Don't worry," Dr. Gardner continued. "Nothing is more important to us than our guests' privacy. We're just thrilled for the opportunity to introduce an alternative method to relationship healing."

"Uh-huh." Matthew digested the kind woman's words and then reached over to close his wife's gaping mouth. "This Sexuality and Liberation program of yours…exactly how does that work?"

Before Dr. Gardner could respond, Chanté finally found her voice. "Excuse us for a minute, won't you?" She grabbed Matthew by the arm and tugged him aside. "I don't care how it works. We're not staying!"

"Oh, c'mon, Chanté," Edie jumped uninvited into the conversation. "Give it a try. What do you have to lose?"

"You, stay out of this!" Chanté jabbed her finger in the center of Edie's breastbone. "What were you thinking tricking us to come to a place like this?"

"We," Edie said as she dragged her groaning husband into the argument, "are trying to help you, since both of you are too proud and stubborn to do the right thing. I mean, really! Duct taping the house, cutting up expensive cars and tampering with food. Does any of that sound like what two rational, mature adults do to resolve conflict?"

"Don't forget what he did to my shoes," Chanté added, crossing her arms with a great huff.

Edie gave her friend an annoyed look as she

slid her hands onto her hips. "Look, Seth and I know you two are a little on the neurotic side. We're your friends. We accept that. We also know you two still love each other."

Chanté lowered her eyes and then stole a side-glance at Matthew. His deep onyx gaze softened as it roamed her face. "A marriage needs more than love."

"Yes, it needs communication and hard work," Edie answered. "Somehow in your crazy quest to always be right, you've forgotten how to connect. You've forgotten how to touch each other."

"Hey, I've tried to connect with her."

"When? In between getting drunk and passing out?"

"I knew that wasn't a dream!"

"No, it was a nightmare."

"Okay. Okay," Edie snapped. "The bottom line is that you guys need help."

The group fell silent.

Finally, Matthew cleared his throat. "I'm willing to give it a try, if you are."

Chanté looked up again, this time her eyes were glossed with unshed tears. "I…guess…we could give it a try."

"Yes!" Edie jerked her arm back as if her favorite football team had scored a touchdown.

Dr. Gardner cleared her throat and everyone turned toward her with guilty smiles for having forgotten she stood behind them.

"Uh, yes. About that program?" Matthew asked again with a widening smile.

Dr. Gardner clasped her hands together and rocked excitedly on the balls of her small feet. "Our Sexuality and Liberation program gives our couples the framework and tools for lovemaking."

"Tools?" Seth asked, and then grinned at his wife. "I'm already liking the sound of this."

Edie smacked him on the arm. "Behave."

"I believe that great sex is a rarity even for couples who are in love. I'm interested in making it a repeatable reality."

"Now I like the sound of that," Chanté said.

Edie turned around and gave her girl a high-five.

Seth frowned and curled his bottom lip. "How come she didn't get smacked?"

His wife playfully smacked his arm again. "Don't worry about it."

"Since you'll be staying," Dr. Gardner chuckled, "how about I show you to your private lodges?" She winked.

Seth and Edie took the lead, linking their arms together.

Chanté and Matthew followed, moving like shy teenagers out on their first date.

The Tree of Life Resort was nestled comfortably in the Sandia Mountains, halfway between Santa Fe and Albuquerque. Walking down the long, curvy multicolored stone walkway, everyone had a breathtaking view of the dusty rose and lavender skyline.

The stunning desert landscape easily transported Chanté back to her Texas days. She nearly laughed at the thought. When had she started thinking of those days as simple?

She looked over at Matthew. At least when they had first gotten together, it had been simple.

Hadn't it? Shaking her head, she concluded that she didn't know anymore.

"Here we are, Mr. and Mrs. Valentine." Gardner slid a card key into a door lock. "I trust you'll find everything to your satisfaction."

Chanté drew a deep breath and fluttered a smile as she crossed the threshold. The southwestern decor continued in their grand lodge. Handsome leather chairs, handwoven coil baskets and even Native American patchwork quilts gave the room an authenticity, but it was the giant stone fireplace that quickened her heart and tickled her imagination.

"Very nice," she said, setting her purse on what appeared to be a hand-carved wooden table.

Matthew nodded his agreement and slid his hands into his pants' pockets.

Dr. Gardner beamed and clasped her hands to her chest. "Great! You'll find everything you need in the folders laid out on your bed. It has your workshop overviews, schedules and instructions. You'll have one class tonight before dinner and then there's a small mixer."

"Great. We get to meet the other couples," Matthew said. "So much for privacy."

"Are you saying you want to leave?" Chanté asked, afraid he was having second thoughts.

"No. No. That's not what I meant…unless—you want to leave."

"No. I mean, we're already here."

Edie rolled her eyes. "Let's leave these two alone, Dr. Gardner. They can go at it for hours. Trust me." She addressed her friends. "See you guys at dinner?"

"Sure. Meet you there," Matthew answered with a smile that didn't quite reach his eyes and then waited patiently for the group to exit.

When the door finally clicked close, he dropped his artificial smile and deflated his shoulders.

"Quite an interesting turn of events," Chanté commented with forced amusement.

"I'd say." Matthew nodded and then failed to think of anything else to add.

Chanté turned and exaggerated her interest in the room's decor. However, her husband's gaze grew heavier on her back while the silence became deafening. Was he expecting her to say something—do something?

"Do you think this will work?" he finally asked when she completed her circle around the living room.

She shrugged. "I don't see why not, it's a fairly large place."

"No. You know that's not what I meant."

He stepped forward and crowded her personal space, but she stepped back when that unfamiliar cologne tickled her nose. "I don't know. In the past six months we've said a lot…we did a lot to hurt each other."

Matthew lowered his gaze and grudgingly nodded. "But it doesn't mean that I stopped loving you," he added tenderly. At her soft gasp, he chanced another look up and watched her beautiful amber eyes fill with tears.

"I still love you, too," she responded in a trembling whisper and closed her eyes. "Do you know how long it's been since we've said those words to each other?"

While his mind tumbled over recent months, Matthew's face heated with shame and embarrassment for failing to do the number one thing he advised the world to do: always tell the people in your life how much you love and appreciate them.

"I'm sorry," he said, taking another step forward.

Chanté blinked. "What?"

"I said I'm sorry. I've been an incredible asshole and you deserve better."

Something certainly had to be wrong with her hearing. Dr. Matthew Valentine had never apologized for anything—not that she should be keeping some sort of scorecard, but it just never happened.

Her husband frowned at her. "Did I say something wrong?"

She shook her head as a few tears skipped down her cheeks. "No. In fact, you said everything just right."

Matthew smiled and erased the remaining distance between them. Their gazes remained locked as his hand cupped her chin and tilted up her lips.

Butterflies emerged from their cocoons and began batting their new wings in the pit of Chanté's stomach. She even held her breath in anticipation as Matthew's head slowly descended. When their lips finally touched, a dam of emotions broke within her soul and tears streamed down her face.

Matthew groaned and pulled her tighter. Despite a surge of urgency and testosterone, he took his time exploring her mouth and dancing with her tongue. What was undoubtedly his millionth kiss from her, this one had every bit of sweetness as their first.

Matthew allowed hope to bloom in his heart. He didn't know what to expect in the next four days, but he vowed to do whatever it took to win his wife's heart back.

Chanté didn't know whether this place could save their marriage but, at least, they were off to one hell of a start.

Outside the Valentines' lodge, Edie and Seth stood with their ears pressed against the door.

"I can't hear anything," Seth complained.

"I think they're kissing," Edie whispered with a widening smile.

"You're kidding me." He pressed his ear to another spot on the door. "I can't believe it," Seth whispered back in genuine amazement. "They're not trying to kill each other."

"Oh, ye of little faith." Edie moved away from the door and pulled her husband along. "You know if this all works out according to plan, we should write a book."

"Yeah. We can name it: *Lie, Sneak and Trick Your Friends to a Happier Marriage*."

"Catchy. I like it."

Seth rolled his eyes.

Chapter 12

Chanté held Matthew's hand firmly as they entered the first workshop of their Sexuality and Liberation program. Edie and Seth were already there, mixing and mingling with the group as if they did this sort of thing every day.

Given the Valentines' celebrity status, most of the participating couples made the assumption that Chanté and Matthew were teaching the course. When they learned the celebrity duo were actually participants, everyone's excitement level increased.

"This experience is going to change your life," Wilfred, a seventy-something gentleman with a George Hamilton tan and a whistling ear aide confided. "This is me and Mable's ninth time here at The Tree of Life Resort," he said, nodding his head vigorously. "Each time we come, we learn something new. Ain't that right, Mable bear?"

Mable, a very tall, Bea Arthur look-alike nodded and expanded her crimson-red lipstick smile. "That's right, Willicums."

"The last time we came, we learned the principles of the Kama Sutra. Now that was fun!"

Matthew and Chanté shared an amused glance before another couple introduced themselves.

"Hello, Dr. Valentine." Jeff, according to his name tag, looking considerably younger than eighteen, pumped his hand. "My wife and I love your show." His wife, though attractive, was three times the boy's age. However, they were clearly crazy about each other.

"I keep tellin' her that age ain't nothin' but a number. Ain't that right, Dr. V?" Jeff went on about his and his wife's winter/spring relationship.

"As long as everyone's legal," Matthew agreed good-naturedly.

Chanté muffled a laugh behind her hand as she turned away and then introduced herself to another couple. In total, there were fifteen couples. Some were newbies and some were veterans. Chanté found that the other couples attended the workshops as a way to either spice up their love life or because they were just plain curious.

"Good evening, everyone," a bald Asian man said upon entering the room. "Please take your seats, so we can get started."

The seats were actually large, multicolored velvet pillows spread in a big circle. Matthew followed everyone's lead by sitting more toward the back of the pillow and then spreading his legs so that Chanté could sit in the vee he formed.

The only couple that alternated from this pose was Wilfred and Mable—mainly because Mable was a whole foot taller than her husband.

Their instructor smiled as he took his place in the center of the circle. "Good evening," he said again. "My name is Dr. Dae Kim. I'm happy to meet each of you as you prepare to embark on a wonderful journey. With our simple techniques you will be transformed. In the next four days, you will learn the ancient art of lovemaking. You will learn how to generate powerful surges of sexual energy."

Mable let out a loud "whoop" and the group crackled in amusement.

Dr. Kim smiled at the elderly couple. "Ah, Mable and Wilfred. Welcome back."

A beaming Wilfred gave the instructor a high thumbs-up. "Wouldn't have missed it for the world!"

Chanté was enchanted by the loving couple. Despite the height difference, they appeared comfortable in their skins and with each other.

"The most important thing I want you to go away with tonight," Dr. Kim continued, "is how through some simple exercises and rituals, sex can be used to heal and free the mind, body and soul. Each one of you can achieve a state of bliss. But first, you must identify past hurts whether they are real or imagined."

Chanté and Matthew shifted in their seats.

"The reason it's important to identify these various hurts, rejections or abuses is because it's the only way to release the emotions attached to them. Once you do that, you then replace those hurts with positive experiences and emotions."

Dr. Kim's words floated inside Chanté's head long after class and dinner. Could she and Matthew truly get past all the temper tantrums and arguments in the past year? Four days hardly seemed like enough time.

The men were excused from the evening mixer so they could get started on their homework. Before Matthew left, Chanté did her best to wheedle clues as to what their mysterious homework entailed.

"If I tell you, then it would ruin the surprise," Matthew chuckled and then kissed the tip of her nose before he left the dining room.

"Stop obsessing," Edie said after reading her friend's pensive expression.

"I wasn't," Chanté lied with a forced shrug of indifference. However, she took one look at her friend's dubious expression and broke out into a wide grin. "This is sort of exciting," she confessed.

"So you forgive me for tricking you?"

Chanté tilted her head high and pretended to mull the question over.

Edie popped her lightly on the shoulder. "C'mon. You two were being stubborn and you know it."

"All right. All right." Chanté swung her arm around her friend's shoulder. "Thank you for caring so much."

"Don't mention it," Edie said, waving off the praise. "I'm sure you would have done the same thing for me."

"If you say so."

The women continued to mill excitedly around the plush room. The Tree of Life staffers didn't miss a trick with surrounding them with various exotic flowers, filling the trays with sinfully rich chocolates and playing soft classical music.

Being that it was ladies' night, waiters who looked like models roamed about the room in scantily-clad genie outfits that boldly and proudly displayed their bulging muscles. Once, Chanté caught sight of seventy-something Mable slipping a twenty-dollar bill in the lining of a young man's waistband and then giggling like a young school-girl.

"You think we'll be like that when we get older?" Edie inquired.

"God, I hope so."

At precisely nine o'clock, Dr. Gardner entered the room, tinkling a small, gold bell. "It's time ladies," she sang merrily. "Each of your husbands or partners has prepared a special evening for you. Tonight, you will be the center of attention. As you learned in class, the pathway to the perfect state of bliss is finding the perfect balance. To give and receive. Traditionally women are givers—the nurturers. And men—well, you know where I'm going with this."

The women laughed.

"Tonight. Your only role is to be the receiver. Abandon your natural instincts. Let your partner pour everything they have into you. Take it all in.

Give your body freedom to move in the way that it wants. Lose control. Do you think you can do that?"

"Yes," the women thundered.

"Good." Dr. Gardner glanced around at the smiling women. "Enjoy your evening." She jingled the bell again.

Before Chanté could set down her flute of champagne, she had to jump out of the way as the women took off like a pack of thoroughbreds at the Kentucky Derby—Edie included. Not that she wasn't equally excited as the others, she was. It was just that she was more nervous than anything.

Which was silly, wasn't it?

Shrugging the question off, she strolled back to her private lodge with an arrhythmic heartbeat and trembling legs. At the door, she fidgeted, drew several deep breaths and finally mustered up the courage to knock.

Immediately, the door flew open and Matthew stood, looking devilishly handsome in a loose, black silk robe. "I was afraid you got lost," he said.

Chanté's jaw slackened at the sight of her husband's broad, chocolate chest and a tease of his rippling six-pack.

He smiled at her reaction and stepped farther back. "Please, come in, my beloved." He gestured with a wide sweeping hand. "I've been expecting you."

Beloved. Chanté tingled from the word as she crossed the threshold. Immediately, a wondrous blend of jasmine and vanilla wafted under her nose and brought a smile to her lips.

Matthew closed the door and then quickly appeared at her side. "May I take your purse and shoes for you?"

Fighting not to laugh, she handed him her purse and started to kick off her shoes when he stopped her.

"No, no. Let me do that for you."

He knelt before her and Chanté's brows shot up in surprise, and then relaxed in delight when he gently lifted one leg at a time to slide off her pumps.

"You have very beautiful feet," he said,

looking up at her. "Would you like for me to massage them for you?"

Chanté couldn't stop grinning. "I'd love a massage."

Matthew stood and put away her things. When he returned, Chanté gasped as he swept her up into his arms.

"You're taking your job a little seriously this evening."

"I hope that doesn't displease you. I am at your service, devoted to your pleasure, my beloved."

Chanté's toe tickled at that word again. "Why would I mind you being my love slave?"

"Ah, that's the spirit," Matthew chuckled as he carried her to the bedroom.

Chanté gasped again at the beautiful sight of low-lit candles, crushed roses on the bed, champagne on ice by a small alcove and a lamp that projected stars across the ceiling.

"You've been busy."

"I hope that means you like it."

"I more than like it," she said, catching his dark gaze. "I love it."

KIMANI PRESS™

An Important Message from the Publisher

Dear Reader,

Because you've chosen to read one of our fine novels, I'd like to say "thank you"! And, as a special way to say thank you, I'm offering to send you two Kimani Romance™ novels and two surprise gifts – absolutely FREE! These books will keep it real with true-to-life African-American characters that turn up the heat and sizzle with passion.

Please enjoy the free books and gifts with our compliments...

Linda Gill

Publisher, Kimani Press

Peel off Seal and Place Inside...

PUBLISHERS
FREE GIFTS
SEAL
THANK YOU

We'd like to send you two free books to introduce you to our new line – Kimani Romance™! These novels feature strong, sexy women and African-American heroes that are charming, loving and true. Our authors fill each page with exceptional dialogue, exciting plot twists, and enough sizzling romance to keep you riveted until the very end!

KIMANI ROMANCE ... LOVE'S ULTIMATE DESTINATION

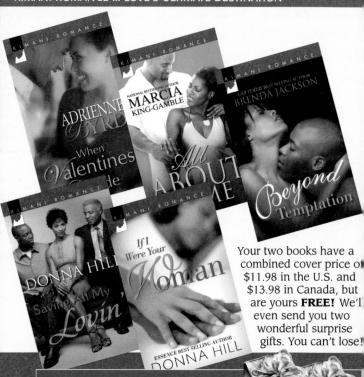

Your two books have a combined cover price o $11.98 in the U.S. and $13.98 in Canada, but are yours **FREE!** We'l even send you two wonderful surprise gifts. You can't lose!

THE EDITOR'S "THANK YOU" FREE GIFTS INCLUDE:

▶ Two NEW Kimani Romance™ Novels

▶ Two exciting surprise gifts

YES! I have placed my Editor's "Thank You" Free Gifts seal in the space provided at right. Please send me 2 FREE books, and my 2 FREE Mystery Gifts. I understand that I am under no obligation to purchase anything further, as explained on the back of this card.

PLACE
FREE GIFTS
SEAL
HERE

168 XDL ELWZ   368 XDL ELXZ

FIRST NAME	LAST NAME

ADDRESS

APT.#	CITY

STATE/PROV.	ZIP/POSTAL CODE

Thank You!

The Reader Service — Here's How It Works:

Accepting your 2 free books and 2 free gifts places you under no obligation to buy anything. You may keep the books and gifts and return the shipping statement marked "cancel." If you do not cancel, about a month later we'll send you 4 additional books and bill you just $4.69 each in the U.S. or $5.24 each in Canada, plus 25¢ shipping & handling per book and applicable taxes if any.* That's the complete price and — compared to cover prices of $5.99 each in the U.S. and $6.99 each in Canada — it's quite a bargain! You may cancel at any time, but if you choose to continue, every month we'll send you 4 more books, which you may either purchase at the discount price or return to us and cancel your subscription.

*Terms and prices subject to change without notice. Sales tax applicable in N.Y. Canadian residents will be charged applicable provincial taxes and GST. All orders subject to approval. Books received may vary. Credit or debit balances in a customer's account(s) may be offset by any other outstanding balance owed by or to the customer. Please allow 4 to 6 weeks for delivery.

If offer card is missing write to: The Reader Service, 3010 Walden Ave., P.O. Box 1867, Buffalo, NY 14240-1867

BUSINESS REPLY MAIL

FIRST-CLASS MAIL   PERMIT NO. 717-003   BUFFALO, NY

POSTAGE WILL BE PAID BY ADDRESSEE

THE READER SERVICE
3010 WALDEN AVE
PO BOX 1867
BUFFALO NY 14240-9952

NO POSTAGE
NECESSARY
IF MAILED
IN THE
UNITED STATES

Neither spoke as Matthew carried her to the small alcove and lowered her onto a bed made of plush, black velvet pillows. Next, he brought over a large basin of warm water.

"Would you like some champagne while I bathe your feet?" he asked.

"I would love some."

As attentive as a maître d' at a posh restaurant, Matthew popped the cork to the champagne and then poured the overflowing bubbly into a thin flute. "For you, my beloved."

She tingled again and accepted the champagne.

Matthew returned his attention to bathing her delicate feet. The feel of his strong hands cupping and massaging the soles had Chanté squirming against the pillows. "If you like, I've also prepared a bath for you."

"This night keeps getting better and better."

"That's the whole idea."

Her smile widened. "In that case, I would love a bath."

Once again, Chanté found herself swept up into Matthew's arms and this time carried into the adjoining bathroom. There, another army of scented candles awaited her and on top of the foam of white bubbles were more crushed rose petals.

Suddenly overwhelmed, Chanté felt tears burn the back of her eyes. It wasn't that her husband had never staged a romantic evening, it had just been so long since he had done so. Between their hectic schedules—his working during the day at the studio, her working at night at the radio station and their writing—such grand romantic gestures were lost in the shuffle.

"None of those," Matthew said, catching her errant tear with the tips of his fingers. "I only want you to feel beautiful…and loved."

"Mission accomplished."

"But we've hardly gotten started. I have a whole evening plan dedicated to pleasuring you." He gave her a conspiratorial wink. "May I unzip your dress?"

Unable to help herself, she leaned up on her toes and pressed a kiss against his lips. "Yes, you may."

Chapter 13

Chanté was in heaven.

Sinking deeper into the tub, she was certain every muscle in her body had turned into mush at the feel of Matthew's hands roaming her body as he took his time bathing her.

"More champagne?" he asked.

His rich baritone seemed deeper than usual and when she opened her eyes, she noticed his onyx gaze was polished with passion. Was he getting as hot as she was?

"I would love another glass."

Like a skilled magician, Matthew produced the champagne bottle, without having left her side, and poured her another glass.

"There is one last place I have yet to clean, my beloved," he whispered. "May I have permission to enter your secret garden?"

Chanté choked on her champagne. "My what?"

Her husband looked as though he was having a hard time keeping a straight face as well. "According to the worksheet we are to use a different vocabulary for body parts."

"And you came up with 'secret garden'?"

"It's not without a certain charm," he said, stroking the small vee of curls between her legs. "Of course, if you don't want me to..." He slowly drifted his hand away.

"No." She grabbed his arm with her free hand. "I didn't say that."

"So that's a yes?"

Suddenly shy, she bit her lower lip and nodded. Their gazes locked as his hands glided languidly up her inner thigh. Though she was expecting the probe of his fingers, she nevertheless sucked in a small gasp as he slid one inside of her.

Matthew set a slow, lazy rhythm that made it difficult for Chanté to hold on to her champagne glass. Without her having to ask, he removed it from her hand.

"How do you feel?" he asked.

"Wooonderful," she moaned, licking her lips and sliding her legs farther apart.

"You look so beautiful right now," he said. "What in the world did I ever do to deserve you?"

"You just got lucky," she joked, but then closed her eyes when he glided in another finger, instantly doubling her pleasure.

"I think you're just about clean," Matthew said.

"No, no. Don't stop," she panted.

"As you wish," he whispered.

Chanté shivered at the feel of his warm breath drifting across the shell of her ear. In the next second, an explosion of lights flashed behind her closed eyes and her body shook with incredible tremors.

"That's it, baby. Let it go."

Quaking in the aftershocks of her orgasm, Chanté stilled Matthew's hand in order for her to catch her breath.

"Do you require any more cleaning, my beloved?"

Still panting, she shook her head. "I think I better climb out of this tub before I drown."

"As you wish." Matthew stood and offered a hand to help her stand.

Chanté accepted his offer and loved how a few of the tub's soapy bubbles slid down her body and how the bathroom's cool air drifted across her skin and hardened her nipples.

This time, her husband magically produced a thick, terry cloth towel and wrapped it around her body as she exited the tub.

"After you," Matthew said, sweeping a hand toward the door.

Excited to see what awaited her, Chanté strolled back into the bedroom and glanced around. The romantic setup still caused her heart to beat in double time.

"If it pleases you, I would love to give you a full body massage."

For the first time, Chanté noticed a massage table at the opposite end of the bedroom. Next to it was a long line of body oils.

"If you keep this up, we may never leave this place," she threatened.

"You'll get no complaints from me," he said, leading her to and helping her up on the table.

At the first drop of warm oil against her back, Chanté teetered on the edge of her second orgasm. But then Matthew's large hands rubbed, caressed and teased her body and she quickly found herself back straddling that edge.

"Has anyone ever told you that you have wonderful hands?" she moaned.

"As a matter of fact, yes," Matthew chuckled. "I ran out and married her as fast as I could."

"Then she is a lucky woman," she joked back, but then her husband's hands stopped their massaging.

"No. I'm the lucky one."

Chanté carefully turned onto her side so she

could look up at Matthew. It had been a long time since she could read his emotions so clearly and what she read took her breath away.

He still loved her.

"Kiss me," she whispered, feeling that she would wither away if he didn't.

A small smile tugged his thick lips. "As you wish."

As his head descended slowly, Chanté stretched forward to meet him more than halfway. The moment their lips touched her body continued to melt lazily on the table.

Matthew wavered on his feet and it had nothing to do with the heady taste of champagne on his wife's lips. In fact, he felt certain it had everything to do with the raw energy transmitting between them. He knew by the way her body trembled beneath him, that she felt it, too.

Determined and eager to give her the best night of her life, Matthew gently repositioned her to lie on her back and then broke the kiss. For long seconds afterward, he maintained eye contact. Her emotions were clearly reflected in her gaze.

She still loved him.

"Would you like for me to continue your massage, my beloved?"

"You're welcome to do whatever you want."

He pressed another kiss against her lips and with a great sigh, reached for another warm bottle of oil. He watched in delight when aromatic oil kissed her skin.

"That smells divine. What is it?"

"Chocolate massage oil."

Chanté slid her finger between her breasts and then tasted the oil. "Mmm. That's good."

"Does that mean it meets with your approval?" he asked with a wicked grin while he rubbed the oil over her breasts.

"I'm not sure. I'd like for you to taste it and give me your opinion."

"As you wish." He met and held her gaze again while he lowered his head.

She sucked in a small gasp as his warm tongue settled over her marbleized nipple, and with slow deliberative strokes, Matthew polished it clean of the oil.

"Mmm. I'm not sure. Let me taste the other one." Matthew stretched over and popped the second nipple into his mouth.

Chanté instinctively arched her back and lolled her head from side to side. While he continued to lick and suck her nipple dry, his hands massaged the oil down her flat belly and even between her legs.

Briefly, she wondered if anyone has ever died from such pleasure. If not, then surely she would be the first.

Matthew's tongue, at long last, trailed away from her glistening nipples, only to explore the valley between her breasts.

But he didn't stop there.

Lower and lower he went, setting off tiny tremors. He even smiled to himself when her breathing quickened to someone running a marathon. He squeezed more oil from the tube and ran his hands down her legs and in between her thighs.

When he finally reached the end of the table, he slid his hands beneath her buttocks and then grabbed hold of her waist so he could slide her down to the edge.

"You know, I think I can get a better taste of it this way," he said huskily and then lowered onto a small chair while settling her legs over his shoulders.

Chanté's eyes widened at the feel of her husband's tongue sliding into her. Then they drifted close as it began moving inside of her. Every thought emptied out of her head and all that was left were these wonderful sensations heating up her body.

Matthew paid particular attention to the hard pearl in the heart of her "secret garden." The strokes were languid at first then accelerated to a pace with which she could hardly keep up.

Vaguely, she was aware of herself moaning, but she lacked the ability to monitor or control how loud she cried. When the pressure started building, she tried to squirm and crawl back up the table.

It was too big and too intense, she realized, but Matthew would not let her get away. "Oh," she cried and then screamed as she tried to brace herself.

However, there was nothing she could've done to prepare herself for the earth-shattering explosion that detonated from one deft stroke of Matthew's tongue.

Chanté discovered a new octave as blinding lights flashed behind her closed eyelids. Shortly after, she struggled for breath and gripped the sides of the table. She arched her body as high she could, trying to break the intimate kiss, but Matthew stood with his tongue still delving deep inside of her, driving her insane.

The pressure began to build again and the squirming and twisting became mindless. She wanted to beg for time to catch her breath, but somehow she'd forgotten how to speak. All she could manage were senseless moans and orgasmic cries. In the next second, another orgasm slammed into her and sent her soaring through an endless sky.

"Baby?"

A lazy smile drifted across Chanté's lips. "Hmm?"

"How do you feel?"

"Like water," she murmured truthfully. Nothing in the world would convince her that he hadn't drained her of muscle and bone.

Her husband's soft laughter danced through the air like music.

She was unaware of being lifted from the massage table, but she was aware of being placed onto the bed's silk sheets.

"I think I've come to a decision," Matthew said.

"Oh?"

"Yeah." He nibbled on her ear. "I love chocolate."

She giggled and lolled her head away.

"Of course," he said, reaching across her. "We could always try the strawberry."

Chapter 14

The next morning, Chanté woke with a smile as wide as a football field and a body completely rejuvenated. Memories from the previous night began to spin lazily inside her head and she released a moan of contentment as she leaned back against Matthew.

Glancing over her shoulder, she smiled when her eyes met her husband's. "Good morning," she whispered.

"That it certainly is." He kissed the tip of her

nose and continued to hold her in their spoon position. "It's been a long time since I've seen that kind of smile on your face."

She twisted around so she could lie on her back and stare up at him. "You know, you're smiling, too, and you wouldn't let me—"

"You weren't supposed to." He kissed her. "Last night was your night. Of course, it shames me to say that after years of training, I never thought to do that for you on my own, to just give a whole night dedicated to you. What does that say about me?"

"That you're not a mind reader," she offered. "You had no idea I was unhappy until I kicked you out of our bedroom. Then I was a crazy woman."

"Amen to that."

"Hey!" She gave his chest a playful shove. "I wasn't the only one who flew over the cuckoo's nest. You're buying me a new car and replacing every shoe you destroyed in my closet."

Matthew laughed and rolled over onto his back. "I really did lose it, didn't I?"

Chanté now moved onto her side and ran a finger down the length of his chest. "I don't ever want us to get like that again."

"You know, I always said that if we had a child—"

She groaned and also rolled onto her back. "What?"

"Nothing," she mumbled, but it was clearly a lie.

Matthew launched back onto his side and took a cue from her by drifting his own finger up her chest and then around her breasts. "That was not a nothing. That was clearly something."

She shook her head, but a thin sheen of tears coated her eyes.

"C'mon, talk to me. We're supposed to be starting over, remember?"

Chanté didn't speak for a long moment, but her husband was determined to wait it out. "It's just that you're always talking about children and…" She shrugged. "Maybe it's not in the cards for us. Maybe we're just not meant to be parents."

He took her hand in his. "Look, I know that we

had our difficulties conceiving, but there are a lot of options we haven't even tried yet. Now that your book is such a success, I was hoping that you would let the radio station go…"

She pulled her hand away and rolled out of bed.

"Where are you going?" he asked.

"It's nine o'clock. We have a ten o'clock class and we haven't taken a shower or had breakfast yet."

"We also weren't finished talking," he pointed out.

"No, no. You're right." She shrugged again. "We still have a lot of options." Chanté flashed him a smile and trotted off to the bathroom where she closed the door firmly behind her.

Matthew fell back against the pillows, wondering what in the hell had just happened. Whatever it was, he guessed that it was somehow his fault. Maybe it was one of those times he should follow Seth's advice and just apologize.

Groaning, he fell back against the pillows. Would he ever understand his own wife?

In the bathroom, Chanté turned on the shower, but she didn't immediately step inside the tub. Instead, she reached for her cache case and pulled out her morning pills. At the sink, she cupped a handful of water and used it to wash the pills down.

When she was done, she stared at her blurring reflection in the mirror. "Quit my job," she mumbled under her breath. "Why does his dream mean I have to give up what's important to me?"

And why can't I just tell him the truth?

She shook her head and turned away from the mirror. Standing beneath the steady stream from the showerhead, Chanté continued to grapple with the question until she heard the shower curtain slide on its rail.

Matthew stepped in behind her wearing a wide smile. "Care if I join you?"

It was just on the tip of her tongue to tell him that it was a free country when she realized that she needed to check herself. Her husband was doing his best to make this four-day excursion work. The least she could do was meet him halfway.

"Actually, it looks like you arrived just in time to help me with my back." She winked.

"As you wish." Matthew grinned and took the loofah from her hand.

She turned and waited while he squirted more liquid soap onto the loofah and then smiled when he began scrubbing her back.

"Uhm, about what happened in the bedroom," Matthew started awkwardly. "I'm sorry if I said something that upset you." He cleared his throat. "I was thinking and, you know, you really don't have to quit your job if you don't want to. I know how much you love it at the station. I was just making a suggestion."

This was the second time in two days that Matthew had apologized and it still had the effect of having the rug pulled out from beneath her. "Thank you," she whispered.

Matthew stepped forward so that her soapy back pressed against his chest. "I just want to do whatever it takes to make you happy."

Tears sprang to her eyes at the complete sincerity in his voice. *Tell him.*

Chanté turned around with the full intent to tell him the truth, but one look in his handsome face, and she simply couldn't do it.

"We'll get pregnant again," Matthew said. "And I'm willing to wait however long it takes."

She twitched her lips into a smile and nodded her head like a good little girl. As her reward, Matthew leaned forward and gave her a kiss that nearly took her breath away.

Matthew and Chanté weren't the only ones late for their morning workshop. Mable and Wilfred, as well as Seth and Edie tiptoed in more than thirty minutes late. Every woman had a certain glow about them that wasn't there the day before, while every man held their chest about three inches higher.

Dr. Gardner, dressed in a bright sun-yellow gown, moved about the room as she lectured about the importance of soul gazing.

"I want everyone to turn on their pillows and face their partners," Gardner instructed.

Matthew and Chanté complied, folding their legs into the Indian position.

"Now, for the next twenty minutes, all I want you to do is stare into each other's eyes. I know it will seem awkward maybe even silly at first, but this exercise is to get you into the practice of truly connecting with your partner. We've all heard the phrase 'The eyes are the windows to the soul.' You need to go beyond just eye color, you need to connect with the soul."

Dr. Gardner was right, Chanté felt silly just staring at her husband. And for the first five minutes, they did little more than give each other goofy smiles.

"Now concentrate on calm, even breathing as you continue soul gazing," the doctor said.

Again, Chanté did as she was told and after a few deep breaths something happened. Her husband's dark gaze somehow felt like an industrial magnet that pulled her into its depth. She grew lightheaded but comfortable at the same time.

Sighing in contentment, Chanté suddenly felt loved. But a renegade question as to whether she was worthy of his love and trust derailed her soul gazing and brought her out of her trance.

"Very good, class." Dr. Gardner clapped her hands together. "How do you feel?"

The crowd murmured different answers while Matthew leaned forward. "That was sort of weird how that worked."

Chanté agreed and returned her attention to the instructor. The class went on to learn the Yab Yum position—where the man sits cross-legged and the female sits on top of his legs and wraps her legs around his waist. Keeping the Yab Yum position, they learned how to transfer each other's sexual energy by leaning close to soul gaze and synchronize their breathing.

By the end of the class, Matthew and Chanté felt less like educated doctors and more like flower children from the sixties.

"How are you liking it so far?" Edie asked Chanté as they sat down for lunch.

"I—it's definitely different," she answered, glancing over at her husband.

"Forget that," Matthew cut in. "I feel like a kid in a candy store."

"You and me both," Seth snickered. "Who knew a woman had so many sex buttons to push?"

"Or that you could push them all in one night," Matthew volleyed.

"Duh," Chanté and Edie intoned together and then slapped each other a high-five.

The men rolled their eyes but knew better than to continue with the touchy subject.

After lunch, the men and women were once again split up, this time to learn different techniques to awaken and honor the god and goddess within them. Overall, Chanté thought it was a fun class and made a mental note to do more research on the subject for possible future books.

"Now's the time for us to discuss this evening's homework." Dr. Gardner beamed at the crowd of excited women.

In response, everyone clapped, except for Mable who shouted, "Bring it on."

"Your assignment, ladies, is to give your partner the best night of his life. Last night, you were just the receiver. Tonight, you will cultivate your natural instincts and become the giver. It's important that you become subservient to his needs. Reassure him that you are there to please him and he does not have to do anything in return. Any questions?"

Everyone shook their heads, but Chanté was already experiencing a mild case of panic. Being an independent woman and always an equal partner in the bedroom, the word "subservient" made her nervous.

"You're obsessing again," Edie said, cutting into her thoughts.

"No, I'm not."

Edie lifted a dubious brow.

"All right, so I was. Sue me."

"What's the matter? I thought that you were having fun?"

"I was—I—I mean, I am." She shook her head. "Don't pay any attention to me. I'm just making things harder than they need to be—as usual." She sighed. "You know, it's not easy realizing that the biggest problem in my marriage is me."

Edie cocked her head to the side. "What do you mean?"

Chanté's talk with her husband that morning flashed through her mind. "Nothing. Forget it. I can do this."

"Well," Edie said, swinging her arm around her shoulders. "Speaking as your friend and not your editor, I'm really happy to see you and Matthew giving this an honest try. As crazy and neurotic as you both are I truly believe that you two are soul mates."

Chanté smiled and also swung her arm around Edie's shoulders. "Despite your lying and scheming, you're the best friend a girl could ever ask for."

"Well said," Edie boasted. "Now what do you say we go and give our husbands a night they'll never forget?"

"Separately, right?"

"Of course," Edie laughed.

"In that case, you're on."

Chapter 15

Matthew couldn't concentrate on the flow of conversation around him during the men's networking hour. Various scenarios of what awaited him had Matt Jr. throbbing painfully against his thigh.

"You're panting like a dog that hasn't had a bone in two years," Seth joked, handing his friend a Heineken. "Calm down, Cujo."

Matt frowned. "Didn't Cujo have rabies?"

"Well, I was going to say Lassie, but she was

a girl. At least Cujo would explain your foaming at the mouth."

"I'm just a little anxious. What time is it?" He glanced at his watch.

"I'm guessing two minutes later than the last time you asked," Seth chuckled.

"Very funny." Matt rolled his eyes because it was exactly two minutes later. He took a swig of his beer. "I have to tell you, man. This trip saved my marriage." He held his friend's gaze. "Thank you."

"Don't thank me. Thank my lovable scheming wife. Frankly, I thought this whole thing would blow up in our faces and I would have lost my best client. I still can't believe it worked."

"Well, so far so good." He looked around. "You know, I should do an exposé on this place and others like it. I'm loving what this whole place is about."

"I'll get on it."

As the hour ticked on at an excruciating pace, Matthew noted that he wasn't the only man glancing at his watch every minute on the minute.

When Dr. Dae Kim jingled a gold bell to draw the men's attention, he made sure to stay away from the door in case of a stampede.

Turns out, there nearly was one and Matthew wasn't ashamed to be the leader of the pack. By the time he reached his private lodge, he was a rocket ready for blastoff.

Calm down. Take a deep breath. He barely tapped the door. The door opened, but his wife wasn't in view. His heart thumped against his chest as he crossed the threshold.

When the door closed behind him, he turned around and then blinked in surprise to see his wife in a sheer white gown. He could see every curve of her body.

"Welcome, my love. I've been waiting for you."

"And I've been going crazy waiting for this moment."

Chanté smiled, but kept her head lowered. "Would you like for me to take off your shoes?"

Matthew pressed his big toe against the heel of his shoes and kicked them off one at a time.

"What shoes?" He then pulled his shirt off over his head, unbuckled his pants and rushed toward her.

This time Chanté couldn't help but laugh and she had to press her hands against his chest to stop him from jumping her bones right then and there. "Slow down, baby," she cooed up at him.

His pants slid off his hips and hit the floor.

She stifled a laugh at his eagerness. "We have all night."

Was it going to take all night to get to the good part? "Yes. Yes. You're right." He smiled painfully.

"Good." Chanté beamed a smile at him. "I prepared something for you in the living room." She started to walk off and then stopped. "Uh, would you like to see it?"

Matthew understood the slip. His wife was not the submissive type, which made him appreciate the effort she was putting into this. "I would love to see it." He stepped out of the pants pooled at his feet and followed her, wearing only his boxers and socks.

She nodded slyly and then escorted him into the living room area. Just like the night before the place was littered with candles, but instead of the clean floral scents, these candles gave the room a more cinnamon and spice smell. On the room's portable radio was the unmistakable music of Miles Davis.

"Would you like to sit down?"

"Don't mind if I do." He settled onto the leather sofa like a king on a throne. Only then did he notice the spread of food on the large, square coffee table.

"Uhm." She cleared her throat. "I was sort of hoping you'd like to sit on one of the velvet cushions." She gestured to the ones on the other end of the table.

"Oh, yes. Of course." He shot back on his feet and raced over to the cushions.

Chanté took a deep breath and tried to remain in character.

Matthew watched in a dreamlike trance as his wife's beautiful silhouetted figure glided toward him. He almost wanted to pinch himself to make sure he wasn't dreaming, but he decided against it in fear that he would wake up.

"Would it please my love if I took off my gown now?"

Hell yes! He nearly laughed aloud at his eagerness. "It would please me very much."

Like the great tease she was, Chanté's hand drifted to the small zipper in the center of the gown and then slid it down one inch at a time.

Matthew couldn't decide whether this was pleasure or torture. Every impulse in his body demanded that he jump up and rip the damn thing off of her. As much as he loved everything he did for her the previous night, it had been pure agony not to satisfy his own carnal desires—and there was no way he could do it two nights in a row.

At long last the zipper reached the end of its track and Chanté parted the sheer gown to proudly display her womanly curves to his greedy gaze. *Mine. She's all mine.*

"Do you like what you see, my love?"

"No." Matthew licked his dry lips. "I love what I see."

Chanté's lips bloomed wide as she allowed the gown to glide off her body. "May I join you on your pillow?"

"You most certainly may."

She stepped forward and placed each of her long cinnamon-brown legs on opposite sides of his hips, pausing just long enough for him to run his hands against them and enjoy their smoothness. She then lowered her naked body onto his lap and assumed the Yab Yum position.

"Comfortable?" Matthew asked, mainly because if he didn't have on his boxers, they would have been joined together.

"Yes," she answered, her minty breath blowing softly against his face. "Would my love like some fresh fruit to whet his appetite?"

"Don't mind if I do."

Chanté reached out to her side and selected a plump strawberry and carefully dipped it into a bowl of chocolate before she brought it to her husband's lips.

As he bit into the juicy fruit, their eyes locked together to do a bit of soul gazing. It was no surprise to Matthew to see so many different layers to his wife. The most dominant trait was her fierce independence, but just below that were layers of uncertainty and even a tinge of vulnerability.

"How is it?" she asked.

An instant smile slid into place. "You know how I feel about chocolate. Both it and the strawberry remind me of you."

Chanté's cheeks darkened even beneath the low candlelight. "Does that mean that you'd like another bite?"

"Yes, to both." He took the rest of the strawberry into his mouth while their gazes remained locked. He allowed her to continue hand-feeding him an assortment of fruit and even a few oysters before she offered him a bath.

The routine was similar to the night before with the exception of him trusting her to give him an old-fashioned shave.

"Don't worry, I used to do this all the time with my father," she assured.

Still, he would have preferred something made

in the twenty-first century, but this night was also about developing and deepening their bond of trust. So in the end, he sat still with his head tilted back while his wife shaved him.

"There. That wasn't so bad, was it?"

Matthew rubbed his hand against his face and was more than a little impressed. "Wow. I should have had you doing this all along." He waited until she put the blade down, and then pulled her into the tub.

Chanté yelped and caused a huge wave of soapy water to splash over the tub's rim and flood the floor. "What are you doing?" she giggled and floundered around until she lay flat against his chest and smiled into his handsome face. "You know, all you had to do was ask me to climb in."

"What—and miss that surprised look on your face?" He blew a cluster of bubbles off the tip of her nose and then leaned in close for a kiss. "I love you."

Her eyes suddenly glossed with tears and she responded in a shaky whisper. "I love you, too."

Matthew looped his arm around her small

waist and drew her back down for another kiss. He took his time exploring and savoring her hot mouth. Despite the tub's cooling water, he grew hard against her body.

Chanté moaned as she stretched her hand down in between their bodies and wrapped her fingers around his shaft. With light, feathery strokes, she moved just her fingers up and down and around the tip.

Matthew, lost in a rapture of soft, silky flesh, continued to arch his erection against the loving strokes of her hands. Meanwhile, he roamed his hands lazily down the blades of her shoulder, then kneaded the skin along the planes of her back, and then finally cupped her firm, yet curvy butt, giving it a gentle squeeze.

She sighed and opened her mouth wider and allowed him to deepen the kiss. His tongue skated over her slick teeth, danced with her tongue, and savored her unique flavor. Nothing on earth tasted this sweet.

He worked his hands in a circular motion—caressing, squeezing and parting her cheeks. In seconds, he set a slow, hypnotic rhythm that Chanté began, rotating her hips to join the fun.

A long groan rumbled in Matthew's chest as his wife's fingers accelerated their strokes and increased his need to be inside of her, but first, he had to make sure she was ready to receive him. Releasing one of her butt cheeks, he glided his soapy hand farther down and then dipped it between the tuft of curly hair between her thighs.

His wife moved as her body quivered against the intimate invasion. Delighted that the slick passageway was just as warm and inviting as her mouth, Matthew navigated another finger inside and began a languid pump.

Chanté stopped rotating her hips and instead rocked against his plunging hand. Almost immediately, her breath became erratic and the soft lapping of the tub's water became just as melodic as the jazz music playing throughout the lodge.

"I need you, baby," Matthew rasped. "I need you right now."

"Yes, love." She moved to climb out of the tub. "Let me get—"

"No. I don't want to get out of the tub." He took his erection out of her hands and held it up straight up so that the tip poked out of the water. "Slide it in for me, baby."

Chanté's lustful gaze met his own while a mischievous smile curled her lips. "As you wish." She reclaimed possession of his hard shaft and inched her body upward and slid her knees to opposite sides of his hips. The porcelain tub made for a tight fit, but she managed the task set before her.

As she eased down his long, throbbing shaft, they moaned together in mutual satisfaction.

Matthew lolled his head back against the tub as he reveled in the unbelievable sensations of her sweet, tight body.

His deep, guttural moans echoed and bounced off the bathroom's tiles as Chanté continued to rise and fall against his powerful thrusts while squeezing her internal muscles. Heavy-lidded, he watched her lustfully through the mesh of his lowered eyelashes and felt his mouth water for the taste of her bountiful breasts bouncing above him.

Pulling up into a sitting position, he pressed her wet body closer, and then drew a pearled nipple into his mouth.

Gasping, she quivered again, but didn't stop rocking her body. As he suckled and polished the black pearl, his wife's hand clawed at his wet back, running her nails over his shoulders and driving him crazy.

With a rarely displayed strength, Matthew planted his feet firmly at the bottom of the bathtub, wrapped an arm around her waist, and propelled their bodies upward with one mighty push from the tub's rim.

Water splashed and ran down from their soapy bodies. Matthew remained careful as he carried his wife out and sloshed through the bathroom. They fell onto the bed not giving a damn about ruining the silk sheets. The only thing that mattered was finishing what they started.

He reentered her body with a long, easy thrust. Her body's warm honey was so unbelievably slick he clamped his teeth together as if it would help him maintain some type of control. Slowly, he moved within her, trying his best to practice restraint but that was shot to hell when Chanté matched his rhythm, thrust for thrust, and then urged him to a faster tempo with her hips.

He was more than accommodating.

Soon, they were rocking at an exhilarating pace and Chanté's cries of pleasure drowned out his own. When she reached the brink of her climax, she tried to inch higher along the bed, but Matthew's hips dogged her trail and he could feel her body explode and tremble around him.

One of her body's tremors detonated his gargantuan climax as he tensed and drove deep, burying his head against her neck and releasing a throaty growl.

Holding him with both her arms and legs, Chanté rocked with him until he quieted and his shaft stopped pulsing. At this moment their bodies and their hearts beat as one. This was how they were meant to be—none of the craziness that had filled their lives in the past few months.

Matthew finally rolled onto his side, but remained welded inside of her. After their hearts returned to a normal pace, he brushed a lock of hair from her eyes. "Whatcha thinking about?"

"You. Us." She fluttered a shy smile. "The last two nights."

His arms tightened around her as he drew in a deep breath. "What about us?"

"I was just thinking about how nice it is to fall in love again."

Matthew met her steady gaze unblinkingly. "Yes, it is."

Chapter 16

Matthew and Chanté made love throughout the night. Each time, the pleasure intensified and strengthened the newly formed bond between them. By the time morning spilled sunlight through the windows, they were no more than two heaps of flesh piled onto each other.

"What time do we have class?" Chanté asked, lacking the strength to even lift her head.

"Who cares?" he groaned. "I may never leave this bed for as long as I live."

She chuckled and then yawned lazily. When she realized that she was still lying on top of him, she asked, "Am I too heavy?"

"Don't even think about moving," he warned and yawned himself. "As soon as I get my energy back, I'm going to make love to you again." Another yawn. "Any minute now."

"No worries, baby. I'm staying right here." She planted a kiss against his chest and drifted off to sleep again.

The next time she opened her eyes, the daylight had softened and there was the unmistakable sound of rain drumming against the windows. Still straddling her husband's hips, she sat up and glanced groggily about the room.

Matthew groaned as his eyes fluttered open. However, a smile quickly slid into place at the sight of his wife's breasts. "Now this is how a man should be greeted in the morning." He reached up and ran his hands over the soft mounds and loved the way her nipples hardened at his slightest touch.

Before he could get the party started, they jumped from the phone's sudden ring.

Matthew frowned. "Who in the hell would be calling us?"

"I'll give you one guess," Chanté said, reaching over and snatching the headpiece off the receiver. "Good morning, Edie."

"Morning? Try afternoon," Edie corrected. "Wait. How did you know it was me?"

"Simple deduction, my dear Watson," she said, laughing and dismounting her husband.

"Wait. Don't go." He reached for her, but she bounced off the bed, leaving him to grasp nothing but air.

"Was that Matthew?" Edie pried.

"No. Denzel Washington," Chanté shot back. "Who else would it be?"

"Then I take it that last night was another success?"

Chanté watched her husband as he stretched lazily among the sheets. "You can say that," she said, as another wave of desire spiraled through her.

"Good," Edie said triumphantly. "I told Seth you were okay, but he thought that I should double-check to make sure that neither of you reverted to your old ways and tried to kill each other."

"Well, he can relax. We're both alive and breathing."

"Just barely," Matthew shouted. "She wore me out!"

Edie "whooped" loud enough for Matthew to hear and the three of them laughed good-naturedly. "All right. Are we going to see you guys for dinner?"

"Dinner?" Chanté glanced around. "What time is it?"

"Two o'clock," Edie sang merrily. "But don't fret. I was told a lot of people missed the morning classes."

"Told?"

"What—you think you're the only ones who can work it all night long? I am the original Energizer Bunny, baby."

Chanté rolled her eyes and quickly disconnected the call.

"Well, what did our self-appointed babysitters want?" Matthew asked, sitting up. "Or should I even bother to ask?"

"Nothing too serious. She was just spying on us and reserving us for dinner." She waltzed over to him on the edge of the bed and popped a squat on his lap. "But I'm starving now." She leaned forward and nibbled on his ear.

Matthew opened his mouth but he was unable to respond with her warm tongue getting him all excited again.

Chanté chuckled at seeing her husband rendered helpless and decided to cut it out—especially if she wanted to eat anytime soon. "You call room service while I go freshen up," she instructed with a departing kiss.

"Ah, we're not going to eat in the nude?"

"We can." She shrugged as she headed toward the bathroom. "But don't you think we should go to at least one class today?"

"The point is for us to have sex. I think we have the gist of it now," he joked. "We just needed a refresher course."

Laughing as she entered the bathroom, she gave him one final reminder to call room service, then closed the door.

Surprised to see just how much water they had splashed on the floor, Chanté retrieved a few towels from the rack and made floor mats out of them before she went about washing her face and brushing her teeth. When she reached inside of her cache case for her morning pills, she stopped.

"What are you doing?" she asked her reflection. She waited as if her mirror image would actually give an answer. If this was to be a new beginning then she needed to start with being honest—and doing the right thing.

Chanté left the pills in her bag, and then turned to the tub to let out the previous night's water and to take a quick shower. When she finally emerged from the bathroom, wrapped in one of the resort's robes, their late lunch was just being delivered to the room.

Matthew, who'd put on a pair of white boxers to answer the door, glanced up. "Hey, honey, we had a note on the door from Dr. Gardner. She wants to schedule a one-on-one consultation. Do you feel up to it?"

"Psychologists seeing psychologists. Maybe Tom Cruise was right and we're all just crazy."

"Or we all just need someone else to talk to."

Chanté lowered her gaze as she slid her hands into the pockets of her robe. "We should be able to talk to each other."

"True," he said thoughtfully. "But when you're dealing with a proud man who finds it difficult to apologize, then talking to him may not be the easiest thing in the world to do."

"Or when you're dealing with a woman who thinks it's easier to leave than deal with a problem." Sadly, she shook her head as she moved over to the sofa. "It's funny. I give millions of listeners and readers advice, but when it comes to me…?"

"Neither of us has claimed to be perfect. It's hard for teachers to be students and for doctors to be patients. We're learning and growing from our mistakes just like everyone else. Sure we have issues. You like to poison people and I like to cut things up. We're perfect for each other."

Chanté laughed and loved him for brightening

her mood. "Hey, did you know that psychologists had the highest rate of suicide?"

"Huh, I thought it was dentists."

Chanté and Matthew emerged from their daylong hibernation to rejoin their group for a class in tantric dance. At first, Chanté thought she would never be able to master the belly rolls and simultaneous hand gestures, but soon, she found the sensual snakelike movements fun and exhilarating.

Plus, Matthew was completely turned on by her efforts.

After class and a pleasant dinner, Edie asked Chanté to join her for a trip to the ladies' room.

"I take it that you want to talk to me about something," Chanté said, checking her appearance in the mirror.

Edie nodded and turned toward her friend with her arms crossed. "Have you told him yet?"

Chanté's genial smile melted from her face. "Told him what?"

"Come on. This is me you're talking to."

Turning away from the mirror, Chanté met Edie's laserlike gaze dead-on. "Not yet."

Edie rolled her eyes with a loud sigh. "Mind if I ask what you're waiting for?"

"I don't know." Chanté's shoulders slumped as she exhaled. "Something called the right moment?"

"He talked nonstop throughout dinner about it."

"I know. I know." She shook her head. "It's just that it's so important to him and after so many...I can't..." She stopped herself and closed her eyes. "He may not forgive me."

"Aww." Edie moved in close and wrapped her arm around her friend's shoulder. "Of course he'll forgive you. He's in the forgiving business."

Chanté had her doubts but didn't voice them. Instead, she lifted her head and wiped a few errant tears from her eyes. "Maybe you're right. Tomorrow we scheduled a one-on-one therapy session with Dr. Gardner. It's as good a time as any to talk about it. Who knows—maybe there's something to this therapist needing therapy thing."

"That's my girl." Edie squeezed her shoulders. "Let's take those men back to our rooms and work up a black sweat, separately, of course."

Laughing, Chanté quickly fixed her makeup and waltzed arm in arm back out to the resort's grand dining room. However, through the rest of their meal, Chanté's reservations and doubts began to pile on top of one another. Soon, she found it difficult to keep her smile angled at the appropriate levels while the beginnings of a migraine throbbed at her temples.

Matthew leaned to her side and whispered, "Honey, are you all right?"

"Huh? What?" She blinked out of her reverie and glanced around the table to see she'd become the center of attention. "I'm sorry, I didn't catch what was said."

"You were rubbing your head so I just asked if you're okay."

"She does look a little pale," Seth noted.

"Oh, it's nothing." Chanté waved off everyone's concern. "It's just a little headache."

"Well, it looks like the sex gravy train has

come to a halt," Seth joked with a whack across Matthew's back. "Looks like you may be the only man not getting good use of those belly dancing moves tonight."

"Seth!" Edie smacked her husband on the back of the head. "Don't be crude."

"What? He knows I'm just joking with him."

"Keep it up and you'll be on the couch." Edie's annoyance melted when she turned her attention to Chanté. "Do you have any Tylenol or anything? I have some in our room, if you'd like some?"

"Actually, I think I have some in my cache case," Chanté said, massaging her pressure points again.

"We should call it a night." Matthew stood and then offered to assist her from her chair.

"Well, maybe I should go take something." She accepted his offer and stood. "I guess we'll see you in class tomorrow."

The group of friends finished their goodbyes and Matthew and Chanté returned to their private lodge. During the entire walk, Chanté practiced the next day's confession in her head, and each time her vision of Matthew's reaction intensified her migraine.

"You really don't look well," Matthew commented as he led her to the bedroom. "Why don't you lie down and I'll go get your medicine and some water for you."

"Thanks," she murmured. "I'm sure I'll be all right in a little while." She eased back against the bed's pillows.

"Don't worry about it, my beloved." He leaned down and kissed the top of her forehead. "The most important thing is to get you feeling better."

Beloved. She really did love it when he called her that. "Thanks, my beloved."

Matthew's eyes lit up at the use of his endearment and he rewarded her with another kiss; this time a light, sensual one that was as effective in curling her toes as well as fluttering her heart.

"Be right back," he promised.

She smiled as she watched him move away from the bed. Lavishing in her love haze, she couldn't quite remember how she'd allowed things to get so bad between them. Now, she just hoped tomorrow's session with Dr. Gardner wouldn't change all of that.

She closed her eyes and tried to lie still until Matthew returned with her pills, but then her eyes flew wide open when she remembered what else was in her cache case.

Matthew stood above her. In one hand he held a glass of water and in the other, her circular compact of birth control pills.

"Why in the hell do you have these?"

Chapter 17

Chanté bolted out of bed like a light and snatched the pills out of her husband's hand, as if doing so would magically make him forget that he'd ever seen them. Once the damning evidence was in her hand, she felt an overwhelming sense of nausea.

"I believe I asked you a question," Matthew said, setting the glass of water down on the nightstand and settling his darkening gaze on her.

She opened her mouth to launch into the prepared speech for the following day's session, but what came out of her mouth instead was, "You weren't supposed to find those."

Silent, he glared as if he enjoyed watching the room's mounting tension choke the living daylight out of her.

Chanté wasn't used to that sort of combat. She much preferred it when there was a lot of yelling and screaming involved. She was in her element in verbal combat and petty revenge tactics.

How did anyone fight silence?

At long last, Matthew turned on his heel and headed toward the closet. It wasn't until he pulled out his suitcase and propped it up on the bed that Chanté's panic hit her at full throttle.

"What are you doing?" she asked.

"I'm packing," he growled.

She rushed toward the bed. "You're leaving?"

He didn't answer.

"You can't leave. W-we have class tomorrow and—and what about our session with Dr. Gardner?"

He stopped and pierced her with another dark glare. "Tell me about the pills."

Her mouth went dry and after a full minute of struggling for the right words, she gave a flat response. "It's complicated."

Matthew clenched his jaw so tight, a singular vein protruded from the center of his forehead. He turned back toward the closet, grabbed the few clothes he had hanging from the rack, and shoved them—hangers and all—into his suitcase.

"Wait. You can't go." She threw the pills onto the bed and started snatching his clothes back out of the suitcase.

Matthew stepped back and slowly settled his hands against his hips. "Tell me about the pills," he stressed evenly.

"Matthew, it's just that… I tried to tell you but—"

"Tell me about the goddamn pills," he roared, reaching out and grasping her painfully around her arms.

Her vision blurred with a sudden rush of tears. "I've been taking them for a year."

The confession was like a hard slap and Matthew's grip tightened on her arm.

"Let go, Matt. You're hurting me."

He released her immediately, but it didn't stop his hands from trembling.

The silence returned and Chanté squirmed fitfully beneath his murderous glare. She made an attempt to reach him through the windows of his soul, but she couldn't journey past the blackness of his stare.

"A year," he finally growled. "All those times we were trying…or should I say *I* was trying to have a child, you were taking birth control pills?"

"Look, Matt, try to understand—"

"Understand?" he roared. "How can I understand anything if you don't say anything? How could you let me believe that we were in this together?"

"We were in it together. It just got to be too much—too many miscarriages and too much heartbreak. I couldn't…I couldn't keep putting myself through that."

"And what about me?" he shouted. "Don't I have a say about any of this? Why wasn't I a part of the decision-making? Or is this another grand standing position that since it's your body, you get to make all the decisions?"

"That's usually how it works," she snapped back, finally feeling her own anger rise.

"Not in a marriage!" He stormed toward her again. "We're supposed to be equal partners. I know how hard it was to lose every one of those pregnancies. I was right there with you, or did you forget? You weren't the only one who'd gotten emotionally attached to each child we created."

"No, but you were the only one who could bounce back in a twenty-four-hour period, wanting to give it another whirl like I'm some freaking machine where you just drop in a deposit and wait for your baby. Well, I'm sorry to inform you but this machine is broken."

Matthew stepped back and shook his head with disappointment written clearly in every inch of his hard features. "Broken, or just giving up?" He searched her face for a true answer. "I would have supported you if you felt you needed a break or even if you wanted to stop trying. The important thing is for me to be included."

She shook her head and ignored the tears that raced down her face. "That's not true. Every time I even hinted that maybe having a child is just simply not in the cards for us, you throw up a brick wall. It's like you don't hear me!"

"Don't give me that garbage! I thought you were seeking support. You never once said 'Matthew, I don't want to do this anymore' or 'Matthew, I think I need to give my body a rest.' You made up your own mind to lie and sneak behind my back." He grabbed his clothes again and started cramming them back into the suitcase.

"It wasn't like that," she insisted.

"Then what was it like?" he challenged.

Being put on the spot like that, Chanté continued to grapple to find the right words.

"Just as I thought. You know, for a talk radio host, you're a woman of very few words."

"It's because I know what I did was wrong. But I couldn't talk to you then."

"Funny. Millions of people have no problem talking to me, but when it comes to my own wife, I'm treated like some kind of stranger." He clamped his suitcase shut and proceeded to zip it despite a few articles sticking out. "I'm out of here."

When he turned and snatched his suitcase off the bed, Chanté raced around him and tried to block his path. "You can't leave. We haven't finished talking yet."

"You had a year to talk to me. Just like you had a year to make me feel guilty that what was happening between us was my fault."

"I thought it was your fault," she said desperately. "Your obsession for a child left me with no room to breathe. It was almost as if you only wanted a child—like I wasn't enough for you. That's why I kept saying that maybe a child wasn't in the cards for us. I needed to hear that us being childless would be okay. That I was enough for you. But you never said it." Her voice cracked as she madly wiped away her tears. "And I doubt that you can say it now."

Another wave of unforgiving silence crashed through the room and Chanté could feel her heart literally tearing in two.

Matthew lowered his head and tightened his grip on his suitcase. "I have to go." He walked around, incidentally bumped her shoulder, but kept moving without an apology.

Chanté closed her eyes and remained rooted in the middle of the room long after the front door had slammed close.

On the fourth day of the retreat, Chanté remained in her private lodge, hoping that Matthew would return after he'd cooled down. However, morning morphed into the afternoon, and then faded into night and she remained sitting alone. Shortly before ten o'clock there was a knock on the door and Chanté raced to open it up, only to have her heart dive back into despair when Edie stood on the other side.

"Oh, it's you," Chanté said.

"Mind if I come in?"

Chanté cringed at the amount of sympathy dripping from her voice, knowing that there was only one conclusion to be drawn. "I take it you already know what happened between me and Matthew?"

Edie hesitated but then slowly nodded her head. "He called Seth last night," she admitted as she cocked her head. "How are you holding up?"

Instead of answering, Chanté stepped back and gestured for her friend to enter. Once she was inside, Chanté closed the door with a soft click and then wrapped herself in her own embrace. "What did Matthew say?"

Edie lowered her gaze and drew a deep breath. "I didn't hear it all. Like I said, he talked to Seth."

Chanté released a long, frustrated breath and marched back over to the sofa. "If you're going to give me the watered-down version, then just forget it."

"That's not what I'm trying to do."

"Then spit it out," she challenged. "You're supposed to be on my side."

"I'm not on anyone's side," Edie corrected.

Her words cut like a knife and Chanté turned her back, feeling like the entire world had ganged up on her. "Fine. Don't tell me. What do you want?" She plopped down on the sofa and refused to meet her friend's gaze again.

"C'mon, don't take your anger out on me. I am your friend."

"A friend who doesn't take sides. Boy, I hit the lottery with you, didn't I?" Chanté immediately regretted her words. "I didn't mean that," she recanted.

"I know." Edie walked over and staked claim to the empty space next to her. "Do you want to talk about it?"

Chanté sucked in a deep breath and she thought the question over. "Actually, no," she said and realized she meant it. "No pity party. I'm going to be a big girl and own my mistakes."

"He's just angry right now," Edie said, determined to comfort her.

"And I'm just hurt."

"Aww," Edie groaned.

She opened her arms to embrace her friend, but Chanté held her hands up and shrank away. "I mean it. No pity party."

True to her word, Chanté didn't shed a tear

that night, or on the plane ride home. Not until she returned home and discovered that Matthew had moved out, did the dam break and tears flow.

Chapter 18

The Love Doctor to write a prescription for a divorce?

Matthew groaned at the Page Six article in the *New York Post* and then tossed it on the floor of his dressing room. In the past two months, the small room had become his primary residence, so it was only natural that the staff and crew would begin to talk. Rumors swirled fast and heavy. He'd even overheard the lighting tech and the sound engineer spinning a wild tale of how he'd

walked in on his wife having an affair. Later that
same day, the makeup artist and head caterer had
flipped it around to be that Chanté had in fact
walked in on him having an affair.

He fired the gabbing four, but that only added
fuel to the rumors. So he gave up and now pretended not to hear them. In truth, he only meant
to stay at the studio for a short while, just long
enough for him to clear his head or rather cool
down. But one day turned into two and then three.
Before he knew it a week had passed and then a
month and now two. And his head was just as
cloudy as the night he stormed out of The Tree of
Life Resort.

If he'd learned anything in his life and career: forgiving was a process. Saying "I forgive you" wasn't
like a magic spell. You didn't wave a wand and
abracadabra, a heart was healed. Betrayal was like
being injected with poison. It could kill or traces of
it could remain in your bloodstream forever.

No matter how many different ways he tried to
look at it, Chanté's actions were an act of betrayal,
but her words still challenged him. His gaze

shifted to his reflection in the vanity mirror. He'd spent another day counseling married couples on the brink of divorce while all the while he felt like jumping out on the ledge with them.

Maybe this was why psychologists had one of the highest suicide rates.

Or was it dentists?

At the light knock against his door, he fought the temptation to shout "go away" and instead invited the person into the room.

"Dr. Valentine. Great show today," Cookie praised, sliding through the door and closing it firmly behind her.

"Oh, thanks." He leaned forward in his chair and retrieved the outline for the next day's show from his dresser. "You're here kind of late," he pointed out.

"Yeah...I, uh, left earlier and then realized that I'd left my PDA somewhere around here so I swung back by." She held up the BlackBerry in question as proof of the tale.

"Glad you found it." He returned his attention back to the outline as a way of dismissing her.

However, she didn't take the hint.

"Uhm. You're here late, too," she commented, inching from the door.

"I have a lot of work to do," he answered, not bothering to look up.

"It kind of looks like you're living here," she continued. "Are you…?"

Matthew's gaze snapped up to meet her gaze through the mirror.

"About you and your wife…" she ventured, ignoring his glare of warning. She reached the back of his chair and lightly ran her fingers across his shoulders.

"Cookie—"

"Because I was thinking that a woman would have to be crazy to let a man like you go," she purred, changing the direction of her hand to glide it through his low-cut hair. "If I was your girl, I'd make sure that you were well satisfied." She leaned forward and brushed her breasts against his back. "Do you know what I mean?"

Matthew watched her performance with a warped fascination and when he realized that she was waiting for him to say something, he did the only thing he could do.

Laugh.

The young intern froze.

He laughed harder.

Slowly, she removed her hands and stepped back. "What's so funny?"

"That you think I need a girl in my life." He swiveled around in his chair to face her. "I am forty-two years old. The last thing I need is a little girl. How old are you?"

"I'm legal," she said, jutting up her chin.

He nodded and told himself to proceed with caution. "Why would a beautiful girl like you throw yourself at a married man?"

Cookie's lips trembled like she was going through an internal earthquake. Next thing Matthew knew, the young intern was spilling every detail of her short, tragic life—an abusive, alcoholic mother, an M.I.A. father, and her one talent of always falling for the wrong guy.

As he suspected, Cookie's shortsighted flirta- tion with him was more about a lost little girl looking for a father figure than any real feelings of attraction. She cried, smiled and even laughed a little bit, and when it was all said and done, Matthew felt good to put Cookie, real name Cassandra, onto a path of healing.

Now, if he could just do that for his own life, he'd be in business.

"Thank you, Dr. Valentine," Cookie said, rising from the small cot in the corner of the room. "I always knew that you were one of the good guys."

Matthew rose from his chair and gave the girl a much-needed hug.

"Hey, Matt." The dressing room door swung open. "I brought you something to eat." Seth glanced up and froze at the sight of Matthew and Cookie with their arms wrapped around each other.

"Seth." Matthew dropped his arms. "What are you doing here?"

"Hello, Shawanda. Welcome back to *The Open Heart Forum*. What's on your heart tonight?"

"I'm just calling to say that you got some

nerve, Dr. Valentine," the caller said with some major attitude.

Chanté had no trouble imagining a woman with her hands on her hips and her neck swiveling like a cobra.

"How you gonna be giving me advice about how to keep my man when you can't even keep hold of your own?"

Chanté took a deep breath and tried her best not to allow herself to be bated. "I take it you're referring to Page Six of the *New York Post?*"

"Damn right, I am." Shawanda's voice rose as she hit her stride. "Here it is in black and white that your husband is gettin' ready to cut you loose. All you highfalutin pop psychologists are a bunch of hypocrites. Up here trying to tell everybody else how to live while your own lives are a raggedy mess."

Chanté and Thad shared a commiserating look through the Plexiglas. "Shawanda, first let me start off by saying that I don't know where the *Post* is getting their information. My marriage is doing just fine," she lied.

"Uh-huh. Then why is my cousin, Cookie, telling me that your man spends every night at his studio? Hell, he's down there right now."

Chanté's heart picked up its beats and threatened to crack through her chest. It didn't bode well that this caller knew more about her husband's whereabouts than she did. "I'm sure most of you know that my husband works long hours to make *The Love Doctor* show a success—not just for the networks but to reach and inspire his audience to have healthy and productive relationships. It's the same thing I strive to do with this show."

"Uh-huh. Did I mention that my cousin is down there with your husband right now— alone—as we speak?"

Seth blinked, stared, blinked and stared some more.

"I, uh, better get going," Cookie said. Her gaze ping-ponged between the two men as she slowly made her way toward the door. "Uhm, thanks again, Dr. Valentine. I really appreciate you being there for me."

Matthew nodded and finally met her gaze again. "It was my pleasure. You just remember what I said."

She smiled, but it died when she glanced at Seth again. "Good night, Mr. Hathaway." Finally, she slipped out of the door.

Seth waited, hoping his friend and client would launch into an explanation as to what he'd just witnessed. Instead, Matthew walked up to him and reached for the container Seth held in his hands.

"Oh, good. Chinese."

"Yeah, I figured you would be hungry and that you might want to…I don't know—talk."

"Thanks," he said carrying the food over to the cot. "You're right. I'm starved."

"You're going to make me come right out and ask you, aren't you?" Seth moved toward the makeup chair.

Matthew opened the box to his sesame chicken and proceeded to unwrap his plastic utensils.

Determined to navigate through the room's thickening tension, Seth sat down and calmly braided his fingers together. "Is there something going on between you and your intern?"

A muscle twitched along Matthew's jaw and when he finally lifted his black gaze, Seth faltered a bit. "I mean, I know things between you and Chanté are still on shaky ground. But…you don't want to travel down the wrong road. You don't want to break…do something you might regret."

"No. I would never want to do something like that," Matthew said evenly.

"Then nothing…?"

"No. Nothing happened." He set his food aside. "And I'm offended you're even asking me such a question."

"First, let me ask you, are we talking as friends right now?"

Matthew looked as if he was weighing the word "friend" very carefully. "Sure. Why not."

"All right," Seth said, adjusting in his chair. "As your friend, don't give me that offended crap. We both know what the scene looked like when I walked in here. And given what you're going through…"

"Given what I'm going through?"

"Yes. What you're going through," he reaf-firmed. "Look, your marriage is a wreck. There, I said it so you can stop pretending otherwise, but it's not going to fix itself. You love Chanté. I know it and you know it. So stop trying to pick a fight with me."

The twitch made another appearance, but this time, Matt hung his head. "Yes. I love my wife…but I don't trust her." After a long silence, he finally lifted his head again. "You don't have to be a psychologist to know that a marriage without trust isn't much of a marriage at all."

Chapter 19

After *The Open Heart Forum's* broadcast, Chanté finally made good on a rain check with Thad. After a full night of dealing with callers trying to give her marriage advice, Chanté wished she could drink something stronger than herbal tea.

"So you didn't tell him that you were on the pill?" Thad asked after she finished giving him the Cliffs Notes version to the destruction of her marriage.

"That's pretty much the gist of it."

"And now that he's gone, you're pregnant?"

"Never let it be said that God doesn't have a sense of humor."

Thad flipped his Yankees ball cap to the back and leaned over their table. "Okay. Correct me if I'm wrong, but isn't this good news?"

Chanté drifted a hand down over her still-flat belly and blinked away the instant sting of tears. "I'm eight weeks along, ten has been my average." She couldn't say it, didn't want to think it, but…

"Hey, hey." Thad pulled all the napkins out of the table's silver holder and shoved them in her direction. "No crying. I don't do well when women start crying."

"I'm not crying," Chanté sniffled, snatching up a few of the napkins and blotting her eyes. "I just have…something in my eye."

Thad nodded but he looked at her like she was sprouting a second head. When she finally managed to gain more control of her leaking eyes and running nose, he relaxed a bit and asked, "You are going to tell him, right?"

"And never know whether he's coming for me or the baby?" She shook her head. "I wouldn't want to pull him away from Cookie the Intern."

"C'mon. You didn't believe that caller, did you?" Thad asked. "Didn't that Shawanda call months ago about stealing her sister's husband and trying to keep someone else from stealing him from her? Hell, it was probably another sister."

Chanté laughed. "I just have this one image of some brother out there that's just being passed down from one family member to the next."

"Maybe it's not a good thing to teach your children how to share."

"Yeah, probably." Her laugh downgraded to a smile, and then finally a frown again.

"Look, if you're really concerned, why don't we just drive over to the studio and see what's going on for ourselves?"

Because I'm afraid it might be true. Instead of saying the words, Chanté shook her head. "I'm not going to chase him down and beg him to come back home." She sighed pitifully. "He's got to want to do that on his own."

"So you're not going to tell him about this pregnancy?"

Chanté moaned over how many times she'd asked herself this very question. "Yeah. I'll tell him, when and if he comes home."

Edie and Seth curled into a tight spoon after another night of sweaty sex. For a long while, Edie was content to just listen to the sound of her husband's deep, even breathing, but serene thoughts soon turned troubled when they drifted to Chanté.

When they'd first returned from New Mexico, a few tabloids had picked up the story about Chanté and Matthew's stay at The Tree of Life Resort. The *National Enquirer* even had a mini-picture of Wilfred and Mable cheesing for the camera as their reliable source. As promised, Edie had the publicity department send out a press release stating that the loving Valentines' stay at the resort was for research on the West's growing fascination with tantric sex.

A half-truth.

However, Wilfred and Mable weren't the only ones who'd reported the major fight between the doctors that had Matthew storming out of the resort before the workshops was completed. Edie had those reports blasted as fabrications.

A downright lie.

In truth, Edie was surprised the Valentines' split remained quiet for as long as it did. Now that it was out, she not only worried about a publicity nightmare or a possible dip in book sales, but she worried for her friend's well-being.

In the past two months, Chanté avoided Edie like the plague. She didn't return calls, messages or even answer her e-mail. If things continued this way, Edie was sure she'd be reduced to sending smoke signals or turn to stalking her friend. The bottom line was clear. Chanté blamed Edie for what happened.

Maybe she was to blame.

"Stop it," Seth said, squeezing her tight and planting a kiss at the back of her head. "I can hear you thinking from back here."

Edie flittered a sad smile in the darkness. "I

should have listened to you and not gotten involved."

"Chanté and Matt again?"

She nodded. "I thought he would've gone back home by now. I mean—yeah, they get a little crazy sometimes when they're fighting, but this stalemate…"

"I know. When I went by to see him tonight—"

"You saw him?" Edie rolled out from the spoon and flipped over to face her husband. "How did he look? What did he say?"

"I've seen him look better," he confessed. "He said he still loved Chanté."

"Well, that's great," she said, clutching his arm.

"He also said that he didn't trust her."

"Oh." She fell silent and tried to imagine her friends breaking up for good, but couldn't manage it. "She just made a mistake."

"A pretty big one."

"What? That she decided to take a break from the physical and emotional pain of losing one baby after another?" Edie said, sitting up.

Seth lazily rolled onto his back and stared

through the room's sparse moonlight to meet his wife's gaze. "This wasn't another shoe shopping decision. It was a decision they both should have made."

"And we all know he would have been dead set against it. He's practically rabid for a child."

"So you knew he'd say 'no' and that makes it okay to lie about it?"

"She didn't lie," Edie reasoned.

"She didn't tell him the truth either," Seth shot back testily. "Is that how things work around here, too? Anything you know I'm against you just maneuver around me?"

Edie didn't answer.

Seth sat up. "You women."

"What the hell is that supposed to mean?"

"What in the hell do you think it means?" He snatched up his pillow. "If a man lies or manipulates a situation to get what he wants, he's a dog, a jerk or an asshole. When a woman does it, there's a perfectly good reason or rationale behind it like, 'her husband would have said no.' Who gave you the right to veto anything?"

"All right. Calm down. This isn't even our fight."

"Isn't it? You're so quick to stick up for Chanté every time you think I may agree with Matthew. Well, let me tell you so that we're perfectly clear on this. I do agree with him. He has every right to be angry and hurt."

"It's been two months!"

"So lick his wounds and get over it? Why? Because when it comes to childbearing all the decisions are left to the woman? My oldest brother, David, and his wife both decided to wait to start a family after he got his computer business off the ground. A year later, his wife grew impatient, came off the pill, without telling him, became pregnant with twins and now there is no computer company. He has to punch someone else's clock in order to provide for his unplanned family."

"This is hardly the same thing."

"Manipulation is manipulation. Dishonesty is dishonesty. Can I understand why Chanté went on the pill? Yes. Can I understand why she didn't talk to her husband, her partner, her supposedly best friend? No."

Edie and Seth came to a stalemate. Both drew in deep breaths in order to calm down.

"Maybe I better just go sleep on the couch," he said, turning for the door.

"Honey, you don't have to do that," she said and reached a hand out from the bed. "We agreed to never go to bed angry, remember?"

After a long stall at the door, Seth finally turned around. "Look, I know this isn't really our argument," he agreed. "But it would tear me up if I thought that there was something in this world you couldn't come to me about, that there is something you would purposely not consult me on. Especially something this important."

Edie climbed out of the bed and joined her husband at the door. "You're absolutely right. And other than a couple…few…some questionable shopping sprees…" She smiled to lighten the mood. "Look, you're right. All major decisions should be discussed as a single unit. I get that. I just want my best friend to be happy."

Seth finally smiled and leaned down to plant a kiss on her full lips, but when he lifted his head, his brows rose suspiciously. "Just how many shopping sprees are we talking about?"

"Oh, honey," she sighed dramatically and then batted her eyes up at him. "You would have just said 'no.'"

His laugh finally deflated the room's tension and he pulled her over to the bed. "That, my dear, just earned you a spanking."

"Ooh. That sounds like fun."

As usual, Chanté arrived home late. After two months, she expected it to get easier to come home to an empty house. Thank God she had Buddy. He actually turned out be a real companion. He was always excited when she came home. Thinking of Buddy made her think of Matthew. She thought about the times Matthew would wait up for her in the living room pretending to work.

Crazy as it sounded, she even missed the elaborate fights they had. What she wouldn't give to find him waiting for her again.

"I was beginning to think you weren't coming."

Chanté gasped and whipped around toward the voice drifting from the living room.

A light clicked on and there sitting in the center of the white couch was her miracle. "Matthew."

"Chanté," he said gravely.

Her thoughts and emotions crashed head-on and Chanté literally felt her knees weaken beneath her husband's pensive stare. Every fiber of her being was happy to see him, her heart pleaded for her to rush into his arms and beg for forgiveness.

However, there was nothing in Matthew's mannerism that suggested he was in a forgiving mood. "I take it you're not here to stay?" The question stretched between them for so long, she didn't think he'd answer.

"No."

The tears rushed down her face before she had a chance to stop them. "Matthew," her voice trembled. "I know what I did was wrong."

He broke eye contact and drew in a deep breath.

"And I'm sorry," she added, easing into the room. "I made a mistake."

"Maybe this marriage was a mistake," he said, finding her gaze again. "Lord knows we don't behave like a married couple and we fight like schoolchildren." Matthew stood up and walked toward a glass vase that was still superglued to the tabletop. He chuckled at the absurdity. "Let's be honest, if I was a caller on your radio show and I described half of the things that we've done to each other, what would you tell me?"

It was Chanté's turn to drop her gaze. "I'm not saying that we're perfect."

"Damn right, we're not."

"And I have never recommended divorce to any caller. I would urge them to get counseling."

"Ha!" He clapped his hands together and it sounded more like a thunderbolt. "We are counselors. So let's just counsel ourselves, shall we?" he shouted. "Well, Dr. Valentine, my wife and I have been trying to have children for the past five years."

"Matthew—"

"C'mon, doctor. We can do this. We're both qualified professionals from good schools."

Chanté stiffened at the slight barb. "Why do you have to be such an asshole?"

"The same reason you have to be such a bitch," he snapped back.

Her hand whipped across his face in reflex and Matthew's head hardly moved from the blow. The sting in her hand raced clear up to her shoulders and the tears continued to flow down her face. "If you're leaving, then leave."

Matthew's jaw twitched, but then he finally turned back toward the sofa and retrieved his jacket. "I'm going to give you your wish."

Chanté lifted her chin. "What's that?"

He stopped and locked gazes with her. "I'm filing for divorce."

Chapter 20

"I was such a blind, self-absorbed idiot," Chanté spat, storming through Edie's front door. "I've lost him for good now."

"Please, come in," Edie mumbled in the wake of her trail, sighed, and then closed the door. Shaking her head and tightening her belt around her plus-size figure, she stopped. Hadn't she lived this moment before?

"Well, it's good seeing you again," Edie said,

following Chanté into the dining room. "I thought you weren't speaking to me?"

"I'm sorry, Edie," she said, collapsing into a vacant chair at the table. "I wanted to call, but I also wanted to hide in my own shell, too." She buried her head in her hands. "I can't seem to do anything right."

Edie slumped into her chair and pushed her breakfast aside. "What happened?"

"Matthew is filing for divorce. And please don't say anything about professional credibility or book sales."

"No. Of course not." She reached across the table for her hand. "Oh, Chanté. I'm so sorry."

"Not as sorry as I am." She sniffed and brushed away a tear before it had the chance to fall. "The thing is, I should be relieved. No more roller coasters of emotions. No more wondering when the big shoe was going to fall. Not that I have any shoes anymore."

Edie gave her hand an encouraging squeeze. "Maybe it's not too late. Have you talked to him?"

Chanté nodded and missed a few errant tears. "He came by the house last night."

"I take it that it didn't go too well?"

"We're as toxic as ever." She smiled but it looked more like a twisted frown. "Before we went to that resort, I was emotionally prepared for a divorce. When I decided to go on birth control, I did it knowing that Matthew would never understand. And I couldn't find the courage to tell him that I wanted to stop trying for a baby. I'd pick a fight for everything else, a classic case of transfer aggression. Then it became a mad race to leave him before he had the chance to dump me.

"Then something happened at The Tree of Life Resort. We connected. It was like...old times. There was no competition, no bitterness—just love. I found out that I still loved him. And I discovered I still wanted to try and give him what he desperately wants."

Edie's gaze followed Chanté's hand as it drifted down to her belly and her brain jumped to a conclusion. "Are you pregnant?"

Chanté shared another sad, crooked smile. "Yeah. Despite the pills."

Edie was confused. "Matthew's filing for divorce knowing that you're pregnant?"

Chanté lowered her gaze.

"You didn't tell him?"

She shook her head.

"But why?"

"Because he would have stayed…and it wouldn't have been for me."

"But, Chanté—"

"Look, one of the hardest things women have to learn is knowing when to let go." She shook her head during a pathetic laugh. "Do you know how many times I've told callers that?"

"Forgive me, but sometimes there's a real fine line between letting go and giving up."

"Not in this case."

Edie pulled away from her friend and slumped back in her chair. "So that's it then?"

"Yeah." Chanté drew a deep breath and willed her courage to return.

"And what about the baby? What if this time—?"

Still afraid to hope, Chanté chose not to answer.

"Chanté, as your friend, I got to tell you that I think you're making another mistake."

"Another mistake?" she echoed.

"I didn't mean it like that."

"It's okay," Chanté assured her, standing up. "I'm a big girl. I can take my lumps. But don't worry. If—and this is a very big if—I'm blessed to carry this child to term I have no intentions of cutting Matthew out. I just want to make sure that he doesn't stay for the wrong reasons."

Edie drew a deep breath. "I can understand that." She stood. "Don't leave. Stay and have breakfast with me. You're eating for two now. Having any weird cravings yet?"

"Well, don't laugh, but I really could go for some tomato soup and marshmallows."

Edie scrunched up her face. "I would never laugh at that. Not now anyway."

Matthew and Seth met at the International House of Pancakes for their favorite selection of Rooty Tuitty Fresh and Fruity pancakes. However, after Matthew announced his decision to file for divorce, the men fell into an awkward silence.

"I know you think I'm making a mistake," Matthew said finally. "And I know the media will have a field day with this."

"I don't care about that," Seth said. "I'll have an official press release sent out later today."

Matthew nodded and absently twirled his pancakes in his strawberry syrup. "This is the right decision, you know."

"I can't answer that for you."

"No. No. I mean, I'm just saying. Given our situation, our history and given what I know about human behavior, we're not normal. This marriage has taken a wrong turn somewhere."

"Look, one thing I can agree with you on is that you and Chanté are a few cards short of a full deck. And now what you're telling me is that cutting up cars and spiking each other's food is okay, but this…"

"Deception?" Matthew finished for him.

Seth lowered his fork. "Forget it. I—I can't help you with this. As your friend, I'll support you in any decision you make. As your agent, I'll get out whatever message you want to the press. And we'll just leave it at that."

Matthew nodded at his pancakes again. After another lengthy silence, he said, "I went to the house last night."

"Yeah?"

"I was going to be strong, lay down the facts and present my case on why I decided to file for divorce. But the minute she walked in, the words jumbled in my head and my heart ached to the point I couldn't breathe. My head flooded with all these memories of how we met, the first time I kissed her, and even the first time we—well, you know."

Seth gave him a crooked smile.

"Then I remembered how much fun we had at the resort. Rose petals on the bed, long bubble baths and body-oiled massages. I wanted to pull her into my arms one second and then in the next, I was baiting her, wanting a good fight."

"So what happened?"

"What do you think?"

"Right hook?"

"I didn't let it show, but it took me half an hour to blink the stars out of my eyes," he chuckled, but quickly grew serious again. "Fighting is a lot easier than dealing with what's really wrong."

Seth smiled. "You know, it seems I heard somewhere that 'couples tend to argue over something safe or superficial as the battlefield while the serious problems are ignored.'"

Matthew recognized the quote. "Now you know I was right."

"It's not always about being right."

"I know. I know. It's also about being able to say you're sorry. I remember."

"Yeah, but did you learn from it?"

"I thought you weren't getting involved?"

"I thought that you had more sense than to end your marriage because your wife can't have children."

Matthew exploded out of his chair. "Shut up! You don't know what the hell you're talking about."

The restaurant's diners swiveled their heads toward the television star and Seth threw his hands up in surrender when he realized that he'd hit a nerve.

"I'm sorry, man. You're right. I shouldn't get involved." But Seth knew at that moment that he was going to get involved. His wife wasn't the only trickster in the family.

Slowly, Matthew slid back into his chair, but he didn't touch his food. Seth's accusation echoed eerily of those Chanté had thrown at him at the resort. What he'd once dismissed as a ridiculous comment now gave him pause. Was he running toward the exit door of his marriage because of the possibility of no children?

Twenty minutes later, the men gave up the sham of eating their meals and requested their checks. While Matthew sank into a gloomy depression, the wheels in Seth's head churned at warp speed.

The men said their goodbyes and as they dispatched to their separate cars, Seth scooped his cell phone from his pocket and called his wife.

"Honey, it's time to throw the deer back into the water."

"Matt and Chanté?" she guessed.

"Yeah. I just finished having breakfast with Matthew."

"Well, Chanté just left here. Baby, she's pregnant again."

"What? Well, that's good news!"

"Not exactly. She's not going to tell Matthew."

"What? But—"

"Wait, before you get started, I agree with her." Edie gave him a brief rundown of Chanté's reasoning for keeping the pregnancy hidden.

"Well, all this tells me is that we need to act fast."

"I'm all ears. What's the plan?"

"We get them to do what they do best—fight."

Chapter 21

For ten weeks Chanté had grown accustomed to waking up with Buddy's butt in her face. It was just another way to fill the empty space on the other side of the bed. It was a poor substitute really, but after so much time had passed, she'd convinced herself that the trick was working.

However, when she opened her eyes this morning, Buddy was nowhere in sight. Yawning, she propped herself up on the pillows and wiped the sleep from her eyes as she glanced around.

"Buddy? Here, boy. Where are you?" When he didn't waddle out from his hiding place, Chanté groaned for having to get up and look for the adorable mongrel. But after searching every inch of the master bedroom, she grew concerned.

The bedroom door was still closed so she couldn't imagine how he could have gotten out. Also, if he had gotten out, she didn't even want to think about how much destruction the little Tasmanian Devil might have caused in other parts of the house.

"Buddy?" she called, opening her bedroom door. "Where are you, boy?" Chanté carefully combed the house and still there was no Buddy.

She heard a car's engine in the driveway and she rushed to the door to see if perhaps she had a dognapper on the premises. Bolting onto the front porch, Chanté slumped in disappointment to see that it was just old man Roger pulling into the drive.

"Good morning, Mrs. Valentine." Roger waved and shut off his engine.

"Morning, Roger." She pulled her satin robe

close and glanced around the property. "You didn't happen to see Buddy out running around when you pulled up, did you?"

"Nah, I can't say that I did." He turned and glanced around the property as well. "I, uh, did see Mr. Valentine leaving a few minutes ago."

Chanté blinked at the news. "Matthew was here?"

"Uh, yes ma'am." Roger stared earnestly up at her. "Looked to me he was in quite a bit of a hurry, too."

"I don't believe him!" She stomped her foot and pivoted back toward the front door. "I've been the one taking care of Buddy all this time. He has no right!" She marched back into the house and slammed the door.

Roger scratched the side of his cotton-white hair, feeling more than a little guilty for lying to the lady of the house, but Mrs. Valentine's good friend had convinced him that the lie was crucial to get the Valentines back together again—well, that and the two hundred dollars she'd slipped into his shirt pocket.

Frankly, he didn't see how kidnapping a dog was going to do much of anything, but then again, he always thought the feuding shrinks were a little off their rockers anyway.

Buddy was having a great time as far as kidnapping went. During his high-speed race across town, he was given new toys to play with and enough dog biscuits to put him in doggy heaven.

"If I get caught during this caper, I want you to tell the pet detectives that you were never mistreated," Edie said.

Buddy gave her a hearty bark and then returned his attention to the dog biscuits.

Thirty minutes later, Edie arrived at the *Love Doctor* studio, still dressed head to toe in black from her morning heist. She quickly found her husband's car and parked behind it. Seth was to meet her at exactly ten o'clock and at one minute after the hour, she was in full panic mode.

At 10:02, she truly envisioned those pet detectives screeching into the studio lot to take her away. What was the time given for dognapping? Would something like that go on someone's permanent records?

Lost in her thoughts about being hauled to jail, Edie didn't notice the petite woman approaching from the rear of her car. At the hard tap against the window, Edie screamed and nearly wet her britches, which then set Buddy off into a barking frenzy.

After a few heart-pounding seconds, Edie placed a calming hand across her heart and rolled down the window.

"Hi, I'm Cookie." The girl jutted a hand into the car. "Are you Mrs. Hathaway?"

"Maybe," Edie said cautiously and slid her large sunglasses up higher. "Why do you need to know?"

Cookie just smiled. "Well, since I know that little fella over there is Buddy, then I'm going to assume that you are Mrs. Hathaway. Your husband is tied up with the producers of the show and he sent me out to meet you."

Edie groaned.

"Don't worry." The young woman winked. "I'm on your side."

Buddy barked and waved his short tail excitedly.

"I guess that means he trusts you. So what's next?"

"Well, I'm going to take our little friend over there and put him in Dr. Valentine's dressing room. The Valentines' groundskeeper just called and said the wife just drove off the property, so we need to get moving."

Edie was out of the car before Cookie could finish her last sentence. They placed Buddy in the box Cookie brought and then covered the top with a thin towel. In true cloak-and-dagger mode, the women stole into the studio by the back door during the taping of the show.

Once, Buddy barked as they were sneaking past the set's caterers. Cookie, unexpectedly, let go of the box and faked a coughing fit. Edie caught the full weight of the box and kept moving—certain that at any moment someone would stop her.

"Sorry about that," Cookie said as she caught up and directed her the rest of the way to Matthew's dressing room. Once they got him inside, they removed the towel and crammed more dog biscuits into the box, and quickly got the hell out of dodge.

* * *

Chanté arrived at the studio lot, breathing fire. She received more than her fair share of stares when she climbed out of her new Mercedes and marched into the studio, mainly because she still wore her satin pajamas and matching pink robe.

She didn't care. She just wanted her dog back.

The moment she walked through the back door of the sound studio she heard the thundering applause echoing throughout the place. She had hoped to reach Matthew before taping began, now she would have to wait for the next commercial break to grab her husband's attention.

"Chanté." Seth walked up and joined her by one of the camera monitors. "What are you doing here?" He glanced around.

"I just need to speak to Matthew for a minute. I'll stay out of the way." She tapped her foot impatiently.

Seth cleared his throat and made another glance around—when he spotted Cookie a few feet away. When she gave him the thumbs-up, he relaxed and waited for the drama to unfold.

On stage, Matthew turned to address one of his guests but caught sight of Chanté offstage. For the first time in his professional life, his mind drew a blank.

"Dr. Valentine?" His guest, a sixty-year-old man who claimed to be addicted to Viagra, waved his hand before Matthew's line of vision and brought him out of his trance. A few minutes later, Matthew cut to a commercial break and quickly exited stage left.

"Chanté, what are you doing here? And why aren't you dressed?"

"Don't play games with me! You know why I'm here. Where's Buddy?"

Matthew stared at her while he waited for her words to make sense. When that didn't happen, he ventured to ask, "Why would I know where Buddy is?"

"Don't play stupid with me. I know you broke into the house this morning and took him," she hissed.

"What? Don't be ridiculous! Plus, who ever heard of breaking into one's own house?"

"Dr. Valentine?" A stage assistant approached cautiously. "We're back on in thirty seconds."

"You don't have the right to take him. You abandoned him, just like you abandoned me!"

More heads whipped in their direction.

"Will you lower your voice," Matthew seethed. "Do you want the whole damn studio to hear you? And I did not abandon you."

"I don't give a damn who hears me. I want my dog back."

"Dr. Valentine?" the assistant urged again.

"I'm coming," he snapped over his shoulder. He returned his attention to Chanté and waved a finger at her. "Stay put. I'll be right back."

Chanté reached for his finger as if ready to snap it off, but he jerked it back in time and rushed out onto the stage.

Seth shrank back but kept his eye on Chanté as she paced around like a caged tiger.

"I thought you said this was going to help them get back together," Cookie whispered into his ear.

"Patience, my dear. There is a method to my madness."

The rest of the show went without a hitch and Matthew thanked his guests for appearing on the show with a wide plastic smile and then rushed off the stage to see what the hell his wife was babbling about.

"Unhand me," Chanté growled when he gripped her arm and proceeded to direct her away from his crew.

He ignored her and continued to tug while flashing his curious crew his famous television smile.

"I just want Buddy back," she growled.

"I don't have him."

"Liar!"

Matthew reached his dressing room and pitched her inside as fast as he could. When he entered behind her, he was sure his eyes were playing tricks on him. The entire room was ransacked and in the center of his cot was Buddy ripping the feathers out of his pillow.

"Buddy!" Chanté exclaimed, rushing over to the dog.

Matthew glanced around the place. "What in

the hell is he doing here? And look what he did to my dressing room."

"Payback is a bitch." She smiled triumphantly. "Isn't that what you told me?"

"You did this on purpose?"

"Oh, will you just give it a rest. I know you were on the property this morning. Roger said he saw you."

Matthew felt like he was tumbling through the Twilight Zone. He couldn't imagine old man Roger lying on him.

"Chanté, I'm only going to say this one more time. I did not take Buddy."

"Then how did he get here? Fly?"

"You must have brought him here," he concluded.

"You're delusional." She picked Buddy up and headed toward the door. "I'd appreciate it if you'd call before you come over. No more just popping up or dropping in."

"Wait a minute. That's my house, too. I'll show up whenever I feel like it."

"I wouldn't try it if I were you." She snatched

open the door. "File your damn divorce but stay the hell away from me and Buddy. You don't deserve us."

Buddy barked in agreement.

When she stormed out of the room, Matthew tried to review what had just happened. No matter how hard he tried, he couldn't make sense of it. Nor should he understand why the memory of rubbing warm body oil all over Chanté kept playing in his mind while they were arguing.

Seth and Cookie had jumped out of the way when Chanté stormed out of her husband's dressing room.

"The method to your madness isn't working," Cookie said.

Seth nodded. "I hate to say it, but I don't think these two are going to make it."

Chapter 22

"**I** needed to hear that us being childless would be okay—that I could be enough for you," she'd said.

Matthew tossed and turned on his pillowless cot, trying to outrun his demons of guilt, but he couldn't seem to move fast enough. Once again, he abandoned hope of a peaceful night's sleep and kicked off the covers. He couldn't go on like this, constantly second-guessing himself and being ruled by his emotions.

Every day he threw himself into his work, trying not to give his hurt or sense of betrayal breathing room to fester. But there were days when it felt like a cancer and other days when he thought he was blowing things way out of proportion.

It was a damn if you do and damn if you don't situation.

However, one question remained. *Can I give up my dream of children?*

The moment he posed the question, his heart rejected it. Why should he have to give up his dream of children when they haven't exhausted all possible avenues—including adoption?

Matthew groaned. Had he just inadvertently proved Chanté's point? He pushed himself up from the cot and paced the room. God, he missed her.

But could he ever forgive her?

He needed to, wanted to, but…

Exhaling a long breath, Matthew realized he needed a longer walk. He slipped out of his dressing room and took a stroll around the studio.

In the last three months, he'd taken this walk around the building's perimeter too many times to count. Each time, he made a mental journey through his life.

Born to a wealthy African-American family was no guarantee of success. His father, an entrepreneurial jack-of-all-trades had just a high school degree and Matthew, the middle child, was not the first to go to college, but he was the first to make it into Princeton. Even after obtaining his Ph.D. in psychology, postdoctoral certification and licensing in marriage and family therapy; Matthew's life didn't truly begin until the day he broke down on a lonely stretch of highway outside Karankawa, Texas, and he walked three miles to Sam's café and met his future wife.

Matthew chuckled aloud at the memory.

After such a long walk, he'd been annoyed the small café didn't have a public phone. The sassy waitress promptly informed him they were a café and not AT&T. A few more witty banters were exchanged and Matthew found himself trying harder to impress the waitress than obtaining roadside assistance. He'd even gone so far as to pay for a sixty-cent cup of coffee with a platinum card.

Chanté was not impressed.

He never did make it to that conference, instead he rented a room in a Norman Bate-ish hotel and returned to Sam's café every day until Chanté agreed to go out with him. To this day, he loved how Chanté never took any crap and could dish out whatever he shoveled her way.

Lord, he missed her.

He took a seat in one of the empty audience chairs and stared up at the stage. In reality, his job was more Hollywood than psychology. Yes, he believed in the advice he pedaled to his guests, but problems couldn't be solved in a fifty-minute show—or during a two-month hibernation.

He stood and circled the studio once again. When he finally returned to his dressing room, it was close to midnight and he was nowhere near ready to try falling asleep. Matthew's gaze fell to the small radio on the dressing table and, despite his vow to stop listening, he turned it on and tuned in to WLUV.

"Hello, it's now midnight, this is Dr. Chanté Valentine and you're listening to *The Open Heart Forum.* Thad, who's our next caller?"

"We have Nicole on line four," Thad said. "She's having relationship problems."

"Hello, Nicole. What's on your heart tonight?"

"Hi, Dr. Valentine." A high, almost childlike voice filtered through the radio. "I'm calling because I'm ready to give up on finding a good man. I swear all the good ones are taken and the ones running around here now are brothers looking either for a sugar momma or their momma period."

Matthew's heart squeezed at the sound of Chanté's soft chuckle.

"I'm sure it's not as bad as all of that."

"Humph! I can tell you ain't been out here in a while. Every man I meet wants to run me through a five-point inspection—my weight, my size, can I cook, clean, be a freak in the bedroom, and a good girl in public? Do I have a good job, a nice car? Will I treat him like a king and not question his authority? If I pass all of that, then he'll move his tired butt into my house, prop his feet up on my coffee table, hog the remote and tell me half a million lies as to why he can't get a job."

Matthew laughed along with his wife at the woman's theatrics.

"Nicole," Chanté began. "Let me guess, you're meeting these men at a club or perhaps online, am I right?"

"How else are you going meet guys now-adays?"

"The good, ole-fashion way. Friends, neighbors, women at your church—people you can rely on to give you good, solid information on a man's character. I'm not saying that you can't meet any good men from the clubs or even online, but you can swing the odds in your favor by shopping for man like you would shop for anything else. Put him through a five-point inspection. If he fails, move on, don't reward him with a key to your apartment." Chanté sighed. "We'll be back after this."

While the show went to commercial, Matthew grabbed his cell phone from its charger. He held the phone for a moment, contemplating whether he should do this or not, but his fingers dialed before he'd arrived at a decision.

The line rang for a full minute and he was just about to hang up when Chanté's producer, Thad, answered the line.

"Yes, I have a relationship problem I'd like to talk to Dr. Valentine about," he said.

"What sort of problem are you experiencing, sir?" Thad asked, putting him through the screening process.

Chanté kept her eyes on the clock. Tonight's shift seemed to drag on forever and her empathy for her callers was at an all-time low. Maybe she needed a little break—finally take Edie up on that book tour she'd promised or something.

Maybe even go home for a visit. Let her parents kiss her boo-boos and make her hot chocolate.

Thad waved and gave a five-second countdown and then the On Air light lit up.

"Welcome back to *The Open Heart Forum*. As you know, I'm your host, Dr. Chanté Valentine. Thad, who's our next caller?"

"On line two, we have Buddy. He's experiencing marital woes."

"Hello, Buddy. You're our first male caller tonight. What's on your heart?"

"I'm having trouble forgiving my wife."

Chanté stiffened. "Uhm, I, uh, see." Her gaze flew to Thad who looked up from his terminal with a question in his expression.

"See, my wife and I have been together for eleven years. Nine and a half were pretty damn good. Wonderful, really. And then just when I thought we were heading to splitsville we had this…reconnection."

Chanté closed her eyes, remembering that connection all too well.

"But then I found out that she was keeping a secret from me."

Swallowing the growing lump in her throat, Chanté managed to croak, "All women have secrets. Was her secret meant to protect you or hurt you?"

Matthew didn't answer.

"There is a difference, you know."

"But one can cause the other," he said gravely.

"Intentions have to count for something." At his continued silence, she added, "My husband used to say that forgiving was a process. Maybe you just haven't processed this long enough?" Chanté held her breath.

"I wish that was true. The worst part is…the thing she accused me of…the possibility of living without…something—may in fact be true."

A tear trickled down Chanté's face. He finally said it. He couldn't live in a childless marriage. She could never be enough for him.

There was a light click over the line.

"Ma—Buddy? Are you still there, Buddy?"

"He hung up," Thad informed her and then addressed the radio audience. "We'll be back after these messages." He cut to commercial.

Chanté snatched off her headset and grabbed her things.

"Where are you going?" Thad asked. "Was that who I think it was?"

"I have to get out of here. Stuff the rest of the hour with a repeat broadcast. I can't keep doing this. I can't keep fighting him. I can't keep begging for forgiveness. If he hasn't filed for a divorce, then I will."

Chapter 23

True to her word, the very next day, Chanté filed for divorce. A few hours later, she packed her things, grabbed Buddy and took a flight back home to Texas. Yes, she was running away from a problem—mainly Page Six of the *New York Post*—but she needed a break and she needed family.

Years ago, when Chanté "married up," as her mother called it, she bought her mom and dad a nice western ranch home—which was a considerable step up from the dilapidated shotgun house Chanté had grown up in.

The moment Chanté pulled her rented Camry into the driveway and saw her mother relaxing on the front porch swing, tears she hadn't known had built up poured down her face.

Within minutes, she was folded snugly in her mother's arms and recounting every detail of the past year.

Alice Morris listened to her only child with a loving patience only a mother had. When Chanté was through, she just continued to hold her until the tears ran dry.

Hours later, at sunset, Leonard Morris pulled his old Chevy pickup truck behind the Camry and found the women still on the porch swing with Buddy curled at their feet.

He lumbered up the stairs with a wide smile. "Is that my baby girl?" After a close-up look at Chanté's red, swollen eyes, his mood took a one hundred and eighty degree turn. "I'll kill him."

"Ain't nobody gonna kill nobody," Alice declared, and gave her daughter's shoulders an encouraging squeeze. "What you're going to do is get Chanté's bags out of the car and take them to the guest room. Chanté, go lie down for a spell while I get supper started." She kissed her daughter's temple and helped her up.

Leonard remained rooted on the porch while he watched the women enter the house. When it became clear that he wasn't going to be filled in on what was going on, he glanced down at the strange dog. "And who the hell are you?"

Buddy barked.

"Well, I guess that's about the only answer I'm going to get tonight." He turned and meandered back down the steps to get his daughter's luggage.

Matthew and the staff had just completed taping. He knew he'd made a mistake in calling into Chanté's radio show. Numerous staffers had recognized his voice and noticed Chanté's emotional response to the caller. The set hummed with rumors and speculation.

Though none of that mattered once he received a call from Chanté's attorney.

Divorce. To separate, divide—permanently.

"All right." Seth breezed into the room. "I just finished the meeting with the producers and I think you're going to like their offer for another five-year contract." He stopped and looked over at Matthew. "Are you all right? You don't look so good."

Matthew gave him a half-chuckle, half-groan response.

"You need to go to a doctor or something?"

"Chanté's attorney called."

Seth straightened.

"She filed."

The small dressing room fell silent while Matthew studied his reflection in the mirror.

"I'm sorry, Matt." Seth placed a hand on his shoulder. "I was really hoping you two would work it out."

"Yeah. I know. Kidnapping the dog was a little over the top though."

"What?" His hand fell from his shoulder.

Matthew's lips sloped unevenly. "Cookie told me this morning. She felt guilty about our fight yesterday."

Seth dropped his gaze and shuffled his feet. "Sorry. I just figured—"

"Don't worry about it. Thanks for caring so much."

"Well, it was either that or slice your car in half."

Matthew laughed. "That might have worked better."

Seth smiled, but remained silent by his friend's side until Matthew stood from his chair and reached for his jacket.

"I gotta get out of here," Matthew said. "Do you mind if we go over that offer another time?"

"Yeah. Sure. Not a problem."

"Thanks, man." He rushed out of the door and made it to his car in record time. The objective was to just drive, clear his head, and wait for the pain in his heart to ease. Instead, he found himself pulling up into his own driveway.

"Oh, hello there, Mr. Valentine."

Matthew glanced down the yard to see old man Roger lumbering up to him.

"Long time since I seen you here," he said

candidly. "My wife said that she'd come up here
with me tomorrow to help get more of the furniture covered, like Mrs. Valentine asked."

"What? Why would she ask you to do that?"

Roger stared at him strangely. "She said that
she was going to be out of town for a few months.
'Course, I just assumed you were going to be
with her."

"A few months?" The words hit Matthew like a
ton of bricks. "Did she say where she was going?"

Roger blinked. "Nah, it's none of my business.
'Course I did find it strange that most of your stuff
was glued to the furniture, and the amount of duct
tape everywhere."

"It was, uh, just a little experiment we used to
do."

Roger scratched his head as his disbelieving
eyes studied Matthew. "Uh-huh. Well, like I said,
it's none of my business." He turned and headed
back to finish trimming the hedges.

Matthew glanced up at the house for a long
time, but then decided not to go in. What was the
point? That part of his life was over now.

He slid back behind the wheel of his car. Again, his objective was to just drive, clear his head, and wait for the pain in his heart to ease. Seven hours later, he arrived in Rochester and on the doorstep of his oldest brother.

"Matthew?" Scott stepped out of his palatial redbrick Colonial. The brothers were the same height and build, despite the ten-year difference between them. "What are you doing here? Do you know what time it is?"

Actually, he didn't. He glanced down at his watch and couldn't believe it was midnight. "I'm sorry. I guess I should have called."

"Are you all right?" Scott glanced over his brother's shoulder to peer at the car. "Is Chanté with you?"

Matthew's heart squeezed as if it was encased in a steel vise. "No. Chanté isn't with me." He couldn't bring himself to meet Scott's gaze.

"Oh." Scott fell silent and then seemed to remember they still stood on the front porch. "I'm sorry. Come on in." He stepped back and allowed Matthew entry and then closed the door behind him.

"Daddy?"

Matthew turned and lit up when he spotted his five-year-old nephew, Bobby, standing in the center of the staircase in his pajamas. "Oh, I'm sorry, li'l man. I didn't mean to wake you up."

"Uncle Matt!" Bobby flew down the rest of the stairs and launched into Matthew's arms.

Matthew spun his nephew around and enjoyed the soft scent of baby powder.

"All right, Mini-Me. Time to go back to bed," Scott said. "It's late."

"But I want to play with Uncle Matt."

"C'mon. You know the rules. I'd already let you stay up an extra half hour to play another game of Deadly Dragons. So say good-night."

Bobby poked out his bottom lip and looked as if he wanted to cry.

"How about if I tuck you in?" Matt said, but shot a questioning gaze over at his brother.

"Yeah! Can he, Daddy?"

Scott drew a deep breath and pretended like his son was asking for a huge favor. "All right, but you have to promise to go straight to sleep."

"I promise!"

"He's all yours." Scott slapped Matthew on the back. "I'll go start us some coffee. Something tells me we're going to need it."

"Black, no sugar," Matthew reminded him and then held Bobby over his head and pretended he was rocket blasting up the stairs.

Bobby giggled the entire way and when tucked securely into his Spider-Man sheets, he used his big, puppy dog brown eyes to get his favorite uncle to read him a story. "Are you going to be here when I wake up?" Bobby asked, yawning.

"That's looking to be a strong possibility."

"So we can play race cars?"

"Yes. We can play race cars. Now go to sleep." He leaned down and kissed Bobby's forehead. "Good night."

"'Night." Bobby yawned, rolled over and went to sleep.

At the door, Matthew stalled and cast another glance over at the bed. He sighed at the curled bundle and slid on an effortless smile.

When he finally returned downstairs, his brother awaited him at the kitchen island.

"I started without you," Scott said, lifting his half cup of coffee. "Which story did he get you to read?"

"Harold and the Purple Crayon." Matthew smiled. "You know your son well."

Scott smiled. "It's not hard. PlayStation, race cars and bedtime stories are his favorites."

"You're a lucky man, bro," Matthew said, reaching for his coffee cup.

"I used to be luckier," Scott said solemnly.

Witnessing his brother's faraway look, Matthew knew Scott was remembering his deceased wife, Barbara. It'd been nearly four years since she was killed in a car accident.

"So tell me what brings you into my neck of the woods at this ungodly hour."

Matthew drew a deep breath, wondering where he should begin.

"Maybe I should ask what you did? Forget an anniversary or a birthday?"

"I wish it were that simple." He sighed and took another sip of coffee.

"I know that sigh. This must be serious." After another beat of silence, Scott added, "C'mon. Spit it out. It's not good for us psychologists to keep things bottled up. Do you know we have the highest rate of suicides?"

"Yeah, my wife brought that to my attention." Taking a deep breath, Matthew finally spilled his guts. Scott had been aware of Matthew and Chanté's attempts to have a child, but his expression reflected his shock at hearing the shenanigans that transpired between the couple in the passing months.

When Matthew finished, Scott remained rooted on his stool, staring at his brother.

"Are you crazy?"

Matthew sighed, wondering what made him think Scott would ever understand his point of view.

"You mean to tell me that you walked out on your marriage because you couldn't have it all? The wife and the two point five children?"

"I know it sounds bad."

"You damn right it does."

"Look, Scott. It's complicated." Matthew jumped to his feet and paced. "Chanté and I planned every detail of our lives—careers, family and retirement. Then suddenly she starts making decisions without me and the next thing I know, all the plans are flying out the window."

"Plans? You want to talk to me about plans?" Scott stood and met his brother's direct gaze. "Barbara and I planned to grow old together. We planned for Bobby to have brothers and sisters and to raise them together."

Matthew dropped his gaze and returned to his stool.

"What are you doing, Matt? You love Chanté. I can hear it in your voice when you say her name. It's in your eyes when you're thinking about her. Fine, she should have told you about the pills, but given what you told me, you didn't exactly create an environment where she could tell you.

"So you and Chanté may never have biological children. Adopt. There are plenty of children in the world who need good, stable homes with parents who'll shower them with love. If that doesn't work out then fine—it's just you and Chanté. Would that really be so bad—to be condemned to a life with the woman you love?

"I envy you. I lost my soul mate. I can't believe that you're so willing to walk away from yours."

Matthew hung his head—ashamed that that was exactly what he was about to do. There was no other woman like Chanté. No one excited his passion, or drove him up the wall like she did. For the last few months he'd tried to purge her out of his system, but nothing had worked. He had waited years to start his family when he had all he needed in Chanté. "I've been a fool."

"Damn right you have," Scott grumbled.

Matthew was on his feet again, pacing. "But what am I going to do? She's filed for a divorce. I don't know where she is. She probably won't ever speak to me again."

"You know, whenever Barbara and I had a bad fight, she would always take off to her parents', her second comfort zone."

"Texas," Matthew said, and then glanced up at

his brother. "You know, I think you may be a better psychologist than I am."

"I like to think so." Scott clapped his hand across Matthew's back. "Now stop being an egotistical, self-righteous son of a bitch and go get your wife."

Chapter 24

An excited Chanté stared wide-eyed at the ultra-sound monitor. At only twelve weeks gestation, she wasn't able to see much, but what she could make out filled her with an indescribable joy.

"I wish Matthew was here right now."

Her mother reached over and squeezed her hand. "You know, we could call him."

At the combination of joy and pain, a tear skipped down Chanté's face. "I will, but just not right now."

"You mean after the divorce?"

Chanté didn't answer but returned her attention to the monitor. For the past three days, her mother and father dropped more than a few hints on how they felt about divorce. The reaction surprised her, because her father once viewed Matthew as unworthy of his daughter's hand. Of course, he felt the same way about every boy who'd ever shown the slightest interest in her.

Every prom, dance or social event always fell on Leonard Morris' gun-cleaning night. When she'd finally introduced Matthew to her parents, her father had enough artillery laid out to outfit a small army. However, Matthew gained respect when he sat down, rolled up his sleeves and proceeded to help him clean the guns.

During the car ride home, Chanté smiled at the memory.

"You know, I always did like Matthew," her mother said, completing the two-mile drive back to the house.

"Really?" Chanté said, remembering the sour

looks and sharp quips. "I seem to remember you saying we were like oil and vinegar."

Her mother parked the car and turned in her seat. "All right. Not always, but certainly by the time you two tied the knot. He was your intellectual match and he certainly knew how to take on your fiery temper. Two passionate people are destined to throw off sparks every now and then. So what? You made a mistake and he's hurt. He'll calm down."

"I'm not going to beg him to love me."

Her mother reached over and touched her shoulder. "Do you really think he doesn't love you? What do you see when you gaze into his eyes?"

Chanté remembered their time at the Tree of Life Resort, where they'd learned the art of soul gazing. She remembered how his eyes were like powerful magnets pulling at her. She remembered the lightheadedness, and the love. So much love.

Chanté turned and climbed out of the car. When she walked through the screen door of her parents' house, Buddy barked excitedly.

"Great! You made it back home," Leonard thundered and flashed a wide, awkward smile.

"Good Lord, Lenny. Why are you hollering? People down the street know we're home now."

"Oh." He took the chastisement. "Sorry about that."

Alice walked over to him and planted a kiss against his cheek. "We have pictures of the—"

"You know, it's almost four o'clock. We're missing that *Love Doctor* show."

"You want to watch the show?"

Chanté rolled her eyes. She knew exactly what her father was up to, and she couldn't say that she was against watching the show. She missed Matthew with every fiber of her being and now that she'd passed the cursed ten-week mark in her pregnancy, she did long to share this experience with him.

She sat down on the sofa, feeling more confused as the day ticked along. Would she actually carry this baby to term? Would it be a boy or a girl? Would it look like her or Matthew? Boy or girl, she would love for the child to have

Matthew's dark, mesmerizing eyes and his smooth complexion.

Swimming lazily through her thoughts, Chanté soon realized her parents were huddled almost near the corner of the room, whispering like a nest of bees.

"What are you guys doing?" She reached for her purse to retrieve the ultrasound pictures. "Dad, do you want to see the—"

"Uh, where's the remote? We better turn that show on before we miss the end," her mother exclaimed as though everyone in the room had gone deaf. "Here it is!" she said, pulling the mighty remote out from the sofa's cushions and clicking on the television.

Instantly, Matthew, handsome as ever in a royal-blue suit, filled her father's beloved sixty-inch screen and seemed to stare directly at Chanté.

"I'd like to thank the audience and the viewers at home for tuning in today," Matthew said. "My goal has been to teach everyone about the powers of forgiveness."

"Humph!" Chanté rolled her eyes and crossed her legs.

"Shhh!" her parents hissed in unison.

Stunned, Chanté blinked and sulkily returned her attention to the television set.

"I'd like to thank my guests, Dr. Margaret Gardner and Dr. Dae Kim from the Tree of Life Resort. I only wish that I'd kept my appointment with you months ago," Matthew said sincerely.

Chanté blinked again and leaned forward in her chair. Matthew had paused and glanced off camera a bit—an uncharacteristic move for him. "I know many of you have by now heard that my wife has filed for a divorce."

The audience "aww"ed at the news.

"I want to take the last few minutes of today's show to talk to you and most importantly to my wife, my soul mate. I decided to reach you this way because I'm not interested in portraying to the world that there is such a thing called a perfect marriage. We go through our ups and downs like everyone else. Sometimes there's pain and hurt and words exchanged that you can never take back, no matter how bad you wish you could. And I wish I could.

"I've known for years through training and experience that you can't plan everything in life. But sometimes it's difficult to get your head and heart aligned. All we can do—all anyone can do—is their best and then just hope for the best. We may never have everything we want in life, but I do want you and only you for the rest of my life. I love you. Won't you please take me back?"

"Oh, my God." Chanté jumped to her feet just as the audience released a thunderous applause. "He said it." She glanced over at her parents. "He loves me! Did you hear that?"

Buddy joined in on her excitement and started barking.

"Yes, baby. We heard. Now what are you going to do?"

"I—I gotta go." She glanced around and snatched up her purse. "I have to get back to New York."

"Are you sure, baby?" her mother asked, walking over to her. "Is this what you truly want?"

"Oh, yes!" Chanté grabbed and hugged her mother. "I love him. I've always loved him."

"I can't tell you how happy I am to hear that."

Stunned, Chanté turned toward the hallway and saw her husband, still dressed in the same blue suit from the day's show and holding a long box. He opened it and inside was a replacement pair of Manolo Blahnik alligator boots.

"What? How?"

"I caught the first plane out of New York after this morning's taping," he said, walking toward her. "Your father was kind enough to hide me in the back room and get you to see the show. Did you mean what you just said? Do you still love me?"

Chanté eased out of her mother's arms and walked on trembling legs toward her husband…and her future. "How could I ever stop loving the father of my child?"

Matthew opened his mouth to speak, but then his wife's words penetrated his brain. The boots fell to the floor. "Child? Do you mean…you're about to…we're about to have a baby?"

"Twelve weeks."

Tears sprang to Matthew's eyes and his arms opened in time to catch his wife when she launched toward him. "Oh, my God. Are we really about to do this?"

"I don't know. But I think we're off to one heck of a start."

Alice and Leonard slid their arms around each other and continued to beam at the loving couple.

He nodded but then added, "No matter what happens, we're in this together for the long haul. Right?"

"Right. No more secrets, duct tape or spiking your breakfast."

"Deal."

Chanté lifted her brows. "You don't have anything to add?"

"Oh." He cleared his throat. "No more chain-saws, cutting up shoes or unwanted dogs."

Buddy barked.

"Except for you, Bud."

"In that case, Dr. Valentine—" Chanté wrapped her arms around Matthew's neck "—I think we're going to make it just fine."

Epilogue

Three years later...

"Welcome back, Mr. and Mrs. Valentine," Dr. Gardner greeted the moment the couple walked through the doors of the Tree of Life Resort. "The Hathaways are already checked in. They informed me you've had another baby since your last visit. Congratulations. Your third, right?"

"Right. Our first girl. Now it's Matthew Jr., Leonard Scott, after my father and Matthew's brother, and the new baby is Victoria." Chanté blushed as she curled into her husband's embrace. "We like to think this place is lucky for us."

"We're here to try for baby number four," Matthew boasted.

"I certainly wish you luck. And I also want to express my gratitude for promoting our resort on your shows. We stay pretty booked throughout the year. We even have a couple of new teachers I believe you know."

"Look, Willy. It's the Valentines," Mable gawked from across the lobby.

The elderly couple rushed over. "Hey, you two lovebirds. I hope you are joining our classes in Tao sex." Wilfred beamed his pearly white dentures. "There are quite a few new positions I think you'd get a kick out of."

"New positions? Then count us in." Matthew winked, and then he looked down at his wife. "Maybe we'll get twins this time."

"Honey, I love you, but don't press your luck."

Essence **bestselling author**

DONNA HILL

If I Were Your
Woman

The second story in the **Pause for Men** *miniseries.*

A messy affair left Stephanie Moore determined
to never again mix business with pleasure. But her
powerful attraction to Tony Washington has her
reconsidering—even though she suspects Tony may be
married. She'll need the advice of her Pause for Men
partners to help her sort out her dilemma.

Pause for Men—four fabulously fortysomething divas
rewrite the book on romance.

Available the first week of February,
wherever books are sold.

KIMANI
ROMANCE™

Where had all the magic gone?

FOREVER, FOR ALWAYS, FOR LOVE

Award-winning author

KIM SHAW

Determined to rekindle the passion in her failing marriage, Josette Crawford undergoes a major makeover. But when life changes threaten to derail her love train, she and hubby, Seth, wonder whether their love is strong enough to keep them together forever.

*Available the first week of February,
wherever books are sold.*

KIMANI
ROMANCE ™

www.kimanipress.com   KPKS0070207

USA TODAY bestselling author

BRENDA JACKSON

The third title in the Forged of Steele miniseries...

Beyond Temptation

Sexy millionaire Morgan Steele will settle for nothing less than the perfect woman. And when his arrogant eyes settle on sultry Lena Spears, he believes he's found her. There's only one problem—the lady in question seems totally immune to his charm!

Only a special woman can win
the heart of a brother—
Forged of Steele

**Available the first week of January
wherever books are sold.**

KIMANI
ROMANCE

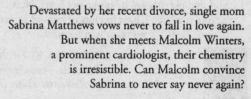